Luc reached for her the moment they were seated in the relative privacy of the car.

His fingers were in her hair, expertly seeking and removing pins as his lips slanted over hers and demanded she open for him. He groaned when she did, the raw and needy groan of a man pushed to his limits, and his tongue began a fiercely sensual invasion, stripping her of everything but the need to respond. Gabrielle wrenched her lips from his and pushed him away with an unsteady hand.

"Drive," she ordered raggedly.

"Where?"

"Anywhere." Although… "Maybe not Caverness." Her courage did not extend to flaunting her intimacy with Luc in her mother's face—not because of what she might think of her, but because Gabrielle feared that somehow, heaven only knew how, she would turn her feelings for Luc into something ugly. "My room."

"Caverness is my home, Gabrielle." His voice was as ragged and strained as hers. "Sooner or later I will want you there." But he drove toward the old mill and said, as they exited the car and strode toward the front door, "I aim to stay the night."

Dear Reader,

Harlequin Presents has always guaranteed seduction and passion, not to mention dramatic and compelling storytelling! And now every month in Harlequin Presents, there are two books that offer you all that you expect from Presents—but with a sexy, flirty attitude!

All year you'll find these exciting new books from an array of vibrant, sparkling authors such as Kate Hardy, Robyn Grady, Natalie Anderson, Kimberly Lang, Nicola Marsh and Anna Cleary. This month, there's the first in Kelly Hunter's saucy new duet, HOT BED OF SCANDAL, set on a French vineyard, entitled *Exposed: Misbehaving with the Magnate*. And there's an exciting and dramatic pregnancy story from hot British talent Heidi Rice in *Public Affair, Secretly Expecting*.

If you enjoy pregnancy stories, don't miss the final installment of Kelly Hunter's duet HOT BED OF SCANDAL, *Revealed: A Prince and a Pregnancy*. And when artist Didi O'Flanagan accepts the commission of a lifetime, she's sucked into a hedonistic life of glamour and luxury in *Memoirs of a Millionaire's Mistress* by Anne Oliver.

We'd love to hear what you think of these novels— drop us a line at Presents@hmb.co.uk.

With best wishes,

The editors

Kelly Hunter

EXPOSED: MISBEHAVING WITH THE MAGNATE

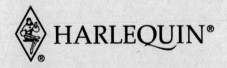

HARLEQUIN®

TORONTO • NEW YORK • LONDON
AMSTERDAM • PARIS • SYDNEY • HAMBURG
STOCKHOLM • ATHENS • TOKYO • MILAN • MADRID
PRAGUE • WARSAW • BUDAPEST • AUCKLAND

Recycling programs
for this product may
not exist in your area.

ISBN-13: 978-0-373-23669-5

EXPOSED: MISBEHAVING WITH THE MAGNATE

First North American Publication 2010.

Copyright © 2009 by Kelly Hunter.

www.eHarlequin.com

Printed in U.S.A.

All about the author…
Kelly Hunter

Accidentally educated in the sciences, **KELLY HUNTER** has always had a weakness for fairy tales, fantasy worlds and losing herself in a good book. Husband… yes. Children…two boys. Cooking and cleaning…sigh. Sports…no, not really, in spite of the best efforts of her family. Gardening…yes, roses of course. Kelly was born in Australia and has traveled extensively. Although she enjoys living and working in different parts of the world, she still calls Australia home.

Visit Kelly online at www.kellyhunter.net.

Two families torn apart by secrets and desire
are about to be reunited in

Hot Bed of Scandal

a sexy new duet by Kelly Hunter
from Harlequin Presents®!

Exposed: Misbehaving with the Magnate—
March 2010

Gabriella Alexander returns to the French vineyard
she was banished from after being caught in flagrante
with the owner's son, Lucien Duvalier—
only to finish what they started!

Revealed: A Prince and a Pregnancy—
April 2010

Simone Duvalier wants Rafael Alexander
and always has, but they both get more than they
bargained for when a night of passion
and a royal revelation rocks their world!

Don't miss this sassy duet!

Available wherever Harlequin Presents is sold

To Maytoners.
And Puppies.

CHAPTER ONE

'BREATHE IN, breathe out,' muttered Gabrielle Alexander as she stood and stared at the daunting wooden door that led to the servants' quarters of Chateau des Caverness. She knew this door, knew the feel of it beneath her palm and the haughty hollow sound the brass knocker made when it connected with the wood. Gabrielle had been sixteen when she'd last walked through this door; sixteen and shattered at the thought of leaving everything she knew and loved behind. Such turbulent times, thought Gabrielle with a wry smile for the girl she'd once been. How she'd pleaded with her mother to be allowed to stay; Lord, how she'd begged and argued and finally wept. But the people she'd loved had not loved her. Josien Alexander had shipped her daughter off to Australia with a heart as hard and as cold as an arctic iceberg.

All because of a kiss.

'It wasn't even a good kiss,' muttered Gabrielle as she stared at the door and dug deep for the courage to put her hand to the knocker and make it do its thing. Seven years had passed; Gabrielle knew a lot more about kissing these days. She knew the feel of hot sweet kisses on her lips. Ragged greedy kisses on her skin. 'It was a very ordinary kiss.'

Liar, said a little inner voice that would not remain silent.

'A practice kiss. A practically meaning-less kiss.'

Big fat liar.

'So shoot me,' she murmured to that little voice inside her. 'You remember it your way and I'll remember it mine.' She grasped the knocker and lifted it. 'Better still, let's not remember it at all.'

But that was harder done than said. Not here in this place, with the scent of summer grapes all around her and the warmth of the sun beating down on her shoulders. Not with her heart swollen and heavy with the knowledge that this place, this chateau, this fragrant idyllic corner of France's Champagne district was the only place that had ever felt like home and that for seven long years she'd stayed away from it.

All because of a kiss.

Taking hold of the brass ring, Gabrielle lifted it and brought it down hard against the wooden door. Boom. Nothing quite like a dreaded sound from her childhood to get her blood pumping and the hairs on her arms standing to attention. Boom. Once more with feeling. Boom boom and *boom*.

But the door did not open. No footsteps echoed along the dark and narrow hallway Gabrielle knew was behind that door. She turned from her mother's quarters to stare across the courtyard at the chateau proper. She *really* didn't want to go knocking on any of those doors.

Josien had pneumonia; that was what Simone Duvalier, childhood playmate and current mistress of Caverness, had said in her phone message. What if Josien was too ill to get out of bed? What if she tried to answer the door and collapsed on the way?

Muttering a prayer to a God she barely believed in, Gabrielle dug in her handbag until her fingers closed around the key she sought. Smooth and cold, it both beckoned and repelled. She had no right to unlock this door—this wasn't her home any more. Caution pleaded with her not to slide the key in the lock but caution never had been Gabrielle's strong point.

Wilful, her mother had called her on more than one occasion.

Headstrong.

Fool.

The key turned easily, smoothly, and with a click and a slight nudge on her part the door swung open. *'Maman?'* Gabrielle stepped tentatively inside the darkened hallway. *'Maman?'* A flash of red caught her eye—red where there'd never been red before. A blinking row of little red lights and a no-nonsense square panel, the kind that signalled state-of-the-art alarm systems that summoned large men with flat top buzz cuts and firearms to the door. *'Maman?'*

And then the cacophony began. No discreet beeping for this alarm system, it was air-raid-klaxon loud and could doubtless be heard for miles. Uh oh. Gabrielle ran towards the blinking lights and wrenched the casing open, staring in dismay at a keyboard containing both letters and numbers. She punched in her birth date. The ear splitting noise continued. She keyed in Rafael's name and date of birth next, but Josien was clearly not the sentimental type. She tried entering the year that Chateau des Caverness had been built, the name and year of its most successful champagne vintage, the number of ancient Linden trees lining the sides of the lane leading up to the chateau, but the alarm just kept on screaming. She started pressing buttons at random. 'Shiste. *Merde.* Bugger!'

'Nice to hear you're still multilingual,' said a midnight-smooth voice from close behind her and Gabrielle closed her eyes and tried to stop her already racing heart from doubling its tempo yet again. She knew that voice, the deep delicious timbre of it. A Champagne voice, a voice of Rheims, it was there in the lilt and the texture of the words. A voice that conjured up forbidden thoughts and heated yearnings. She'd heard it in her dreams for years.

'Oh, hello, Luc.' If he could do deadpan, so could she. Gabrielle turned slowly and there he stood, looking every inch the head of a Champagne dynasty in his tailored grey trousers and crisp white business shirt. Gabrielle could have spent a lot longer staring at Luc Duvalier and cataloguing the changes time had wrought in him but circumstances and a healthy respect for her eardrums dictated moving right along. 'Long time no see. I don't suppose you could help me turn this thing off?'

He brushed past her, long, strong fingers moving swiftly over the panel. *'Cinq six six deux quatre cinq un.'*

The alarm cut out abruptly and silence cut in. A loud, ringing kind of silence.

'Merci,' she said finally.

'You're welcome.' Lucien Duvalier's perfectly sculpted lips tightened. 'What are you doing here, Gabrielle?'

'I lived here once, remember?'

'Not for the past seven years, you haven't.'

'True.' Now that quiet had been restored, Gabrielle could look her fill. She studied the tall, dark-haired, dark-eyed man standing before her, trying for detachment and failing miserably. Luc had been twenty-two when she'd last seen him and even then the promise of tightly leashed power and outrageous sexuality had hovered about him like a velvet cloak. Night, the household staff had called him. And Rafael, Luc's childhood partner in crime, with his fair hair and his teasing blue eyes, had been Day.

'Sorry about setting the alarm off,' she said with an awkward shrug. 'I should have known better than to use the key.'

Luc said nothing. He never had been one for small talk. But it was all she could manage. Taking a deep and steadying breath, Gabrielle tried again. 'You're looking well, Lucien.'

When he still made no reply Gabrielle looked past him, across the courtyard towards the chateau tucked snugly into the terraced hillside. 'Caverness is looking well too. Cared for. Prosperous. I heard about your father's death a few years back.' She didn't feel inclined to say any more on the subject. Had she wanted to lie through her teeth she could have added something about being sorry to hear of old man Duvalier's demise. 'Guess that makes you king of the castle now,' she added recklessly. She met his dark burning gaze without flinching. 'Should I kneel?'

'You've changed,' he said abruptly.

She certainly hoped so.

'You're harder.'

'Thank you.'

'More beautiful.'

'My thanks again.' Gabrielle held back a sigh. If Luc wanted to categorise the changes in her, she might as well show him the big ones. She wasn't a gangly sixteen-year-old on the cusp of womanhood any more. And Luc wasn't the centre of her life. 'Look at us,' she chided lightly. 'Childhood playmates and here I've greeted you with less warmth than one would greet a stranger. Three kisses, isn't it? One for each cheek and then a spare?' She moved closer and brushed his left cheek with her lips, breathing in the subtle pine scent that clung to his skin and trying very hard not to let it wrap around her and squeeze. 'One.' She pulled back and made for his other cheek, never mind that he stood as if turned to stone. 'Two,' she whispered and let her lips linger a fraction longer this time.

'Back off, angel.' Luc's voice was nothing more than a dark and dangerous rumble as his fingers came up to caress her jaw before sliding around to the base of her neck. 'For your own sake if not for mine.'

A warning. One she would do well to heed. Not that she did. A frisson of awareness slid down her spine and she closed her eyes the better to diffuse it. So he could still make her body ache for his touch. Nothing to worry about. She was older now. Wiser. She knew better than to lose her heart to the head of the House of Duvalier. Not that a few more iron clad reasons to ensure she kept her distance from this man wouldn't come in handy. 'Are you married these days, Luc?'

'No.'

'Celibate?'

'No.'

'Are you sure?' She brushed his ear lobe with her lips. 'You seem a little…uptight. It's just an innocent greeting.'

The fingers at the base of her neck tightened. 'You're not innocent.'

'You noticed.' She pulled back smoothly, dislodging his hand with a shrug as she stepped away and shot him a careless smile for good measure. 'You always were observant. Perhaps two kisses *are* greeting enough for you, after all. Shall we take a rain check on the third?'

'Why are you here, Gabrielle?'

Here in this place where no one wanted her. Luc couldn't have made the implication clearer if he'd painted it on a sign and hung it on the door. 'Simone phoned and left a message. She said my mother had been ill. She said…' Gabrielle hesitated, unwilling to reveal any more weakness to this man. 'She said that Josien had been calling for her angels.' Whether Josien had been calling for her children, who'd been named after two of the winged entities, was anyone's guess. Rafe thought not. Rafael thought Gabrielle's decision to travel halfway across the world on the strength of a fevered plea a colossal mistake but even so… Even if Josien refused to see her…

Some mistakes were unavoidable.

Gabrielle attempted a nonchalant shrug. 'So here I am.'

'Does Josien *know* of your expected arrival?' asked Luc quietly.

'I—' Nervously, Gabrielle fiddled with the cuff of her stylish cream jacket. 'No.'

Luc's gaze grew hooded and Gabrielle thought she saw a flash of something that looked a lot like sympathy in their depths. 'You always were too impetuous for your own good,' he murmured. 'I gather your brother declined to accompany you?'

'Rafe's busy,' she said guardedly. 'As I'm sure you must be. Luc, if you could just tell me where to find my mother…'

'Come,' he said, turning abruptly and heading for the door. 'Josien is staying in one of the suites in the west wing until she recovers more fully. A nurse attends her. Doctor's orders. It was that or the hospital.'

Pulling the door closed behind them, and pocketing her keys, Gabrielle hurried to match Luc's long loping stride. 'How bad is she?'

'Frail. Twice, we thought we'd lost her.'

'Do you think she'll want to see me?'

Luc's features hardened. 'That, I have no idea. You should have called ahead, Gabrielle. You really should have.'

Gabrielle's apprehension grew claws as they entered the chateau through the western door. Josien Alexander had always been a mystery to her children. Never loving, constantly critical. Gabrielle had spent most of her childhood trying to please a mother who could not be pleased. Gabrielle's overriding instinct was still to please her, even after seven years of barely any contact with her mother at all. What if Josien didn't want to see her? What if she hadn't been calling for her children at all? What then?

The nurse who met them in the sitting room of the suite was a grizzle-faced man in his mid fifties whom Luc introduced as Hans. Hans had a firm handshake, a steady gaze, and a warm smile for Gabrielle.

'Stubbornest patient I've ever had,' he said. 'She's just taken her medication so you've about five minutes before she begins to get drowsy. Not that she won't fight the sleep. She always does.' Hans gestured towards yet another closed door. 'She's in there.'

'Thank you.' Gabrielle's nerves were at breaking point and her body felt weary beyond belief, courtesy of the twenty-three-hour flight from Sydney, but this was the path she'd chosen to follow and follow it she would, no matter what Rafe thought, or Luc thought, or *anyone* thought. Gabrielle had come to see her mother.

Some mistakes were unavoidable.

'Would you like me to accompany you?' asked Luc quietly.

'No.' Luc's offer of support scraped at her, shamed her. Some humiliations were best kept private. Then again, maybe this meeting *would* go more smoothly with a third party present. With Luc present, Gabrielle amended with brutal honesty, so that Josien could *see* that, as far as Luc was concerned, the mistakes of the past had been paid for. And they had been paid for, hadn't they? Surely they'd been paid for? 'Yes.'

Luc's lips curved ever so slightly. 'Which is it?'

Gabrielle's gaze met his and skittered away. 'Yes.'

'Four minutes,' said Hans dryly.

'Thanks.' Steeling herself, Gabrielle reached for the handle to yet another closed door and headed inside. It was warmer in here. Darker too, for the afternoon light had to pry its way through two layers of gauze curtain material before finding entry. A large four poster bed dominated the space so that the figure tucked beneath the fluffy white bedcovers looked tiny in comparison. Seven years ago, Josien Alexander's hair had been as black as a raven's wing and had fallen almost to her waist. Now it was streaked with silver and cut to sit just beneath her chin but she was still the most beautiful woman Gabrielle had ever seen. Josien's eyes— those startling violet blue eyes that had always watched and judged but never smiled—were closed, and Gabrielle was grateful for the reprieve. She needed that moment to bind her emotions tight.

'Josien,' said Luc gently. '*Pardonnez-moi* for the lateness of the hour but you have a visitor.'

Josien turned her head and slowly, slowly, she opened her eyes, focussing first on Luc, and then on Gabrielle standing awkwardly beside him. With a swiftly indrawn breath, Josien closed her eyes and turned away.

Gabrielle felt the sting of bitter tears welling in her own eyes but she blinked them away, and made herself speak even though her words would come out ragged and choked. 'Hello, *Maman.*'

'You shouldn't have come.' Josien kept her face averted.

'So people keep telling me.' Luc's face, when Gabrielle glanced his way, was as hard and unyielding as the stones from which the chateau had been built. 'I hear you've been unwell.'

'*Ce ne'est rien,*' said Josien. 'It's nothing.'

It didn't look like nothing. Luc had been right. Her mother looked frail. 'I brought you a gift.' Gabrielle reached into her bag for the album of photos she'd put together so painstakingly. Rafe would kill her if he knew how many photos of him she'd included in the mix, but he didn't know and she wasn't about to tell him. 'I thought you might like to know what Rafe and I have been doing these past seven years. We bought a broken vineyard, *Maman,* and brought it back to life. We've done so well. Rafe's a brilliant businessman. You should be proud of him.'

Josien said nothing and Gabrielle felt her lips tighten. So what if Rafael had eventually gone as far away from Josien and this place as he could get? That was what people did when raised on a diet of scathing criticism interspersed with icy indifference. Rafe had never deserved any of the treatment Josien had dealt him. He really hadn't. 'I'll leave it here on the end of the bed in case you want to look at it some time.'

'Take it and go.'

Yeah, well. That was what you got when you believed in tooth fairies, happily ever after, and mothers who actually cared. 'I've taken a room in the village, *Maman*. I'll be in the area these next few weeks. I know you're tired right now but maybe when you're feeling better you could give me a call. Here.' She fished a business card from her handbag. 'I'll leave you my number.' Gabrielle's words were met with more silence. Gabrielle bit her lip—praying for one pain to subdue another, but Josien's rejection had cut too deep. She should never have come here. She should have listened to Rafe and to Luc instead of listening to her heart. 'So…' Gabrielle felt the world sway, and then Luc's hand was beneath her elbow, fragile purchase against the darkness threatening to engulf her.

'Jet lag,' murmured Luc. It wasn't jet lag causing her to sway and they both knew it, but he afforded her the courtesy of an excuse for her body's reaction and Gabrielle seized it.

'Yes. It's been a long day.'

'Wait for me outside,' he said as he gently shepherded her towards the door. 'It's about to get longer.'

Luc waited until the door clicked closed behind Gabrielle before turning to the woman in the bed. Josien Alexander was an enchantingly beautiful woman and always had been. Coolly unfathomable, she ran the housekeeping staff at the chateau with an iron fist and no second chances. She'd raised her children the same way. Luc had bowed to Josien's will all those years ago because he'd seen the sense in sending Gabrielle away, but he saw no sense in Josien's actions now. All he saw was pain.

Josien's eyes were still closed as Luc strode back towards the bed but he didn't need her eyes, only her ears. 'My father told me of our duty to you before he died,' he said grimly. 'I've done my utmost to honour it. I've tried my damnedest to make allowances for your behaviour, Josien, but, so help me, if you don't make time for your daughter while she's here you can pack your bags and leave this place the minute your health allows it. Do you hear me, Josien?'

Josien nodded, tears tracking noiselessly down her cheeks, and Luc struggled to contain his frustration and his fury. 'You've never been able to see it, have you? No matter how badly you wound them or how hard you try to push them away…you just don't get it.' He looked at the photo album and his roiling emotions coalesced into a tight ball of anger directed squarely at the woman in the bed, no matter how fragile or beautiful she was. 'You've never been able to see how much your children love you.'

Luc caught up with Gabrielle halfway along the hallway. He needed a drink. The thorn he'd never quite managed to extricate from his side looked as if she needed one too. 'In here,' he told her, and ushered her into the library that doubled on occasion as his formal office space, usually when he entertained clients and wanted to impress. 'Where are you staying?' he asked as he headed for the bar, reached for the brandy and poured generously.

'In the village,' she replied, careful not to let her fingers brush his as she took the half full glass from his outstretched hand and downed it in a single gulp. 'Thanks.' Her gaze went to the label on the bottle and her eyes widened. 'What…? For heaven's sake, Luc! This stuff has to be at least a hundred years old and expensive enough to make even you wince. You might *warn* a person before you handed it to them. I could try *tasting* it next time.'

'Where in the village?' He poured her another shot. She could taste it now.

'I took a room above the old flour mill.'

'I'll have someone collect your bags,' he told her curtly and downed his own brandy before setting the glass back on the counter somewhat more forcefully than necessary. Gabrielle flinched at the sound. She looked jittery, strung out. She looked like he felt. 'You can stay here,' he told her. 'There's room enough.'

But Gabrielle shook her head. 'I can't,' she said with a stubborn tilt to her chin that he remembered of old. 'You heard her.' Gabrielle smiled bitterly and swirled the brandy in her glass. 'She doesn't want me here.'

'When last I checked,' he said, his voice deceptively mild, 'Luc, not Josien, was master of Caverness. There's room for you here. There's no need for you to stay in the village. Simone, I'm sure, will be glad of your company.'

'And you?' Gabrielle lowered the glass from her lips, and pinned him with a grey-eyed gaze that held more than a hint of pain. 'Will you be glad of my company too? There was a time when you couldn't wait for me to leave.'

'You were *sixteen*, Gabrielle. And if you don't know the reason behind my encouraging you to finish growing up elsewhere then you're not nearly as smart as I thought you were. One more week and I'd have had you naked beneath me. In your bed or mine or halfway up the stairs, I wouldn't have cared,' he said bluntly. 'And neither would you.'

He'd surprised her. Shocked her. He could see it in her eyes. 'Well, then…glad we cleared that up.' She took another sip of her brandy and set her glass carefully on the bench, as if even that small motion took up all of her control. 'I suppose I should thank you.'

But she didn't.

'I lost my virginity to a handsome Australian farm boy when I was nineteen,' she said in a low, ragged voice. 'He was charming, and funny, and he made my pulse race and my body ache for more of him. He was everything a girl could wish for when it came to her first time, and it still wasn't enough.' Gabrielle headed for the door. Luc stood rooted to the spot. 'I'll be staying at the old flour mill for the next three weeks. If you could send word to me if my mother's condition changes, I'd be very grateful.'

'Why wasn't it enough?' Luc's throat felt tight, the words came out raspy, but he had to know. 'Gabrielle, why did he disappoint you?'

He didn't think she was going to answer, but then she turned as she reached the door and speared him with a glance that held more than its share of self-mockery. 'I really don't know. Maybe he just wasn't you.'

Luc waited until she'd shut the door behind her before he let his curses fly. He was a man who took pride in his self control. He'd worked hard for it; fought against his deepest nature to secure it. Only one woman had ever made him lose it. The results had been disastrous for all concerned. Josien had been hysterical, his father aghast, and Gabrielle…innocent, trusting Gabrielle had been exiled.

She'd lost her virginity to a handsome Australian.

Fury roared through him as he picked up his glass and flung it at the fireplace, his temper only marginally appeased when the glass exploded in a burst of glittering crystal shards.

CHAPTER TWO

'YOU shouldn't have said that.' Gabrielle had a habit of talking to herself whenever she felt stressed. She'd been talking to herself ever since she'd set foot back in France. Her footsteps made a crunching sound as she hurried across the gravel courtyard towards her hire car, every step taking her further away from Caverness and the people in it. She needed to leave before she broke down completely. She needed to leave this place *now*.

Gabrielle made it back to the village without mishap. She drove on the correct side of the road and didn't lose her way. She even observed the speed limit. And when she got to the old mill house she locked herself inside her room before finally giving in to weariness and sinking back on the bed with her forearm across her eyes, as if by blocking her sight she could block out the memory of her conversation with Lucien. 'You should *not* have said that.'

It had been seven years since she'd last seen Luc. Seven years of complete indifference on his part. No phone calls, no letters, no contact. Not once. A sixteen-year-old girl had deduced from Luc's actions that he'd simply been playing with her when he'd kissed her all those years ago. That the housekeeper's daughter had meant nothing to him.

Not once, not *once*, had it ever occurred to her that Luc had been trying to protect her from a relationship she'd been nowhere near ready for.

Still wasn't ready for if her recent reaction to him was anything to go by.

So she had money behind her now, and self-esteem, and a good deal more to offer a man on an intellectual level. That still didn't equip her to deal with the likes of Luc Duvalier. Luc, whose brooding black gaze could make her forget every ounce of self-preservation she'd ever learned.

How many minutes in his company had it taken her to test the strength of her physical reaction to him? Two minutes, or had it been three? How long had it taken her to lay herself bare for him? Telling him that her first lover had been a disappointment to her. Gabrielle groaned and rolled over onto her side, burying her head in a pillow and pulling the blue chenille bedspread around her for comfort. What kind of woman told a man that?

A woman who'd never quite forgotten the ecstasy and the agony of a single stolen kiss, said a voice that would not be silenced.

A woman who'd known all along that no one at Caverness would bid her welcome and mean it.

A fool.

Luc didn't usually wait impatiently for his sister to return home from her work, but this day he did, seeking Simone out in the kitchen, never mind the box of fresh fruit and vegetables in her arms or the fact that she hadn't yet managed to put the box down.

'*Bonjour*, brother of mine,' she said cheerfully. 'I come bearing good food and even better news. The sales figures are finally in and we,' she said, setting the bags on the counter with a flourish, 'had a *very* good quarter.'

'Congratulations,' he said, but something in his voice must have alerted Simone to his turmoil for she turned sharply, set the box down on the bench, and took her time looking him over.

'Something's wrong,' she said warily. 'What is it?'

'Josien had a visitor this afternoon.'

'Who?'

'Gabrielle.'

Luc watched his sister's face light up with wry resignation. Simone and Gabrielle had been close as children. Closer than sisters, never mind the huge gap in social standing between them. 'Gaby is here?' asked Simone. 'Here as in here at the chateau? Where?'

'Here as in staying in the village, and before you start in on my manners, yes, I offered her a room, which she declined. Dammit, Simone! Why didn't you warn me that you'd sent for her? And why the hell didn't you tell Josien?'

Simone's expression grew guarded. 'I left a message on Gaby's answering machine saying her mother was ill. That's all I did. What was there to tell?'

'You knew she'd come,' muttered Luc darkly.

'I thought she'd call first.'

'Well, she didn't.'

'So what happened?' asked Simone warily.

Luc gave it to his sister straight. 'Josien wouldn't talk to her. Wouldn't even look at her.'

A barrage of swear words followed his announcement, none of them becoming to a lady. 'So then what happened?' demanded Simone. 'Did *you* make Gabrielle feel welcome?'

'Sort of.'

'Sort of? For heaven's sake, Luc, you're a grown man! Would it have killed you to behave like one?'

'I did behave like one,' he said grimly.

Simone halted, midway between the fridge and the counter. 'Oh, hell,' she said. 'You still want her.'

Luc didn't deny it. What he didn't reveal to his sister was just how intense his desire for Gabrielle had been. He'd barely been able to control it. And he needed to. 'Gabrielle needs a friend right now, Simone, and it can't be me,' he said gruffly. 'I don't want to do wrong by her again.'

Simone's gaze softened. 'Dear heart,' she said. 'The way I remember it, you've never done Gaby wrong. Others have—most certainly they have. But not you.'

'You're a little biased,' he said.

Simone smiled. 'Only a little.'

'She's staying at the old mill house,' he offered next and exhaled his relief as his sister upended a wicker basket full of oranges onto the counter and hastily started refilling it with a variety of foodstuffs from the refrigerator. 'You're going after her?'

'Of course I'm going after her,' said Simone. 'Isn't that what you want? Somebody has to make her feel welcome.'

Gabrielle woke to the sound of vigorous pounding on her door. She sat up with a groan, slung her legs over the side of the bed, and pushed the heavy fall of dark curls from her face before checking her wristwatch for the time. Eight p.m. French time and the early hours of the morning by Australian reckoning. She'd slept for almost three hours. Now she'd never get back to sleep for the night. 'Who is it?'

'Simone,' said yet another voice from her past, albeit a voice currently heavy with impatience. Gabrielle went to the door and unlocked it gingerly before swinging it open. She didn't know if she could cope with any more blasts from the past today. Between them, Luc and Josien had proved quite sufficient. She stared for a moment at the elegant raven-haired beauty in the navy-blue suit, trying to reconcile the image of cool sophistication standing before her with the hoyden that had been Simone. And then she saw the magnum of champagne in the woman's left hand and the basket full of delicacies at her feet and knew that the hoyden was alive and well beneath those daunting designer clothes.

'Look at you, sleepyhead,' said Simone, and Gabrielle found herself enclosed in a warm and perfumed embrace. 'I couldn't believe it when Luc told me you'd come home. Why didn't you call me? I'd have picked you up from the airport. I'd have made all the arrangements. Oh, look at you!' Tears gathered in Simone's expressive brown eyes. 'I always knew you'd grow to be even more beautiful than your mother. It was always there. In your eyes; and in your heart.' Simone pulled back. 'Luc told me what happened with Josien, Gaby. I could *strangle* her. Josien *did* call for you, I swear she did. I thought she wanted to make amends. I'd have never left that message for you otherwise. Never.'

'I know,' said Gabrielle. 'I knew my welcome would probably be somewhat…cool. But I came anyway. You must think I'm crazy.'

'No,' said Simone gently. 'Not crazy. Hopeful. I made us a picnic,' she said, stepping back to the door to retrieve her basket. 'And I don't care where we eat it.' She hefted the magnum up to eye level to reveal the label. 'The day you left I stole two bottles of our oldest and finest and hid them in the caves. I swore on my sainted mother's grave that the day you returned we would drink one of them. Of course, I never expected you to stay away so *long*. What kept you?'

Gabrielle felt her lips curve, she couldn't help it. Finally, a welcome without restraint. 'I was busy growing up and carving out a life for myself in Australia,' she said dryly. 'And I want to know what you're saving the second bottle for.'

'You'll see,' said Simone. 'About this picnic… Shall we eat it here on the bed or shall we dine somewhere where we can see the clouds? We could head for our old picnic spot.'

'So we could.' Gabrielle eyed Simone's attire sceptically. 'You look every bit the successful businesswoman you always vowed you'd be, but are you sure you'll be able to walk up the track in those shoes without breaking your neck?'

Simone looked down at her stiletto-clad feet and frowned. 'You're right. I really hadn't thought this through. Luc shoved me out of the house so fast I forgot to change clothes.' She stared at the small double bed, then cast her eye around the poky little room. 'I lied. I do care where we eat and this isn't the place. We'll have to go back to Caverness so I can change clothes.'

'No,' said Gabrielle hastily. 'No way. I'm sorry, Simone. I'll meet you up at our picnic spot if you like, but I've had enough of Caverness for one day.' If Gabrielle went back to the chateau right now she'd only start throwing things again. Namely herself. At Luc.

'It's just a house,' said Simone, and, at Gabrielle's level stare, 'Okay, a castle. A very big castle.'

'No.'

'I'll smuggle you in and smuggle you out,' said Simone. 'Just like the old days. No one will ever know.'

'Luc would know.' He'd always known.

'All right then,' said Simone. 'Let's approach this like rational, sensible, intelligent women. I'll just borrow your clothes and get changed here.'

'I like it,' said Gabrielle. 'But I'm warning you I shopped for clothes in Singapore on the way over and had to sit on my suitcases to get them to shut. There's wreckage within those cases that I'm not sure you're ready for. There's chaos in there that I'm not sure *I'm* ready for.'

'Unleash it,' said Simone, and released the champagne cork quietly and without spilling a drop of the precious liquid. 'I live for chaos.' Setting the magnum on the bedside table, Simone began to rummage through the basket at her feet. 'I could have sworn I put some champagne flutes in here somewhere. Special picnic ones.'

'Plastic ones?' said Gabrielle.

'Don't be ridiculous,' said Simone. 'Heathen. Where have you been *living* these past seven years? Ah, here they are.' She brandished them aloft with a flourish. 'Not plastic. Polish crystal. Perfectly shaped, beautifully balanced, and as delicately made as petals on a rose. *Plastic* champagne flutes,' muttered Simone with a shudder as she filled the two glasses and handed one to Gabrielle. 'God help us and welcome home.'

* * *

They ate atop the highest hill in the area, surrounded by grapevines and with the rooftops of the chateau spread out below them, and, in the distance, the rooftops and church spires of the village.

'What will you do while you're here?' asked Simone after the last crumbs of cheese had been nibbled and the last sliver of pâté had been devoured. 'Luc said you planned to stay in the area for a few weeks.'

Gabrielle nodded. 'I came here on business as well as to see *Maman*. Rafe and I make wine these days.'

'Oh?' said Simone, her voice a little too offhand to actually *be* offhand. 'What kind of wine?'

'Cabernet sauvignon, mostly, and some cabernet merlot. For the high end of the market and worth every cent. We're looking to extend our export opportunities into Europe and set up a distribution arm. It makes sense to look for premises in the place we know best.'

'Rafael wishes to return?' said Simone.

'No. Not Rafe. Just me.'

'Oh.'

'Don't sound so disappointed.' Gabrielle slid Simone a sideways glance.

'I'm not disappointed,' said Simone with

a toss of her head. 'Not at all. I'm just… curious. What kind of operations base are you looking for? Business premises or residential property?'

'Both.'

'With or without land attached?'

'Depends on the land,' said Gabrielle. 'Why?'

'The old Hammerschmidt vineyard is on the market,' said Simone. 'The vines are in a dreadful state, the winemaking equipment is fifty years out of date, and the house needs a lot of attention, but the cellars are good and the location is excellent. Luc's been looking into acquiring it.'

'Really?' said Gabrielle dryly. 'And you're telling me this why?'

'Because it would probably suit your purposes.'

'If it did I'd be in direct competition for the property with Luc.'

'Really?' said Simone airily. 'Could be fun.'

'For whom?' said Gabrielle. 'Seriously, Simone, I appreciate your help but where's your sense of family duty? Your loyalty to Luc and to your family business? There was a time you put loyalty to family before your own happiness. Where did *that* Simone go?'

Simone's expression grew shuttered. 'That Simone grew up to regret not holding tight to her happiness with both hands. I'm older now. Wiser.'

'Trickier,' murmured Gabrielle.

'That too.' Simone sipped at her champagne and stared at the valley spread out before her, half of which she owned. 'So how is he?' she said tentatively. 'Rafael.'

'Driven,' said Gabrielle with a wry twist of her lips.

'Is he happy?'

'I really don't know.'

'Is he married?'

'No.' Gabrielle took pity on her childhood friend and gave her the information she sought. 'He's had a few relationships over the years. Less than he could have had. Nothing he ever put before his work.' Gabrielle sipped at her champagne. 'He's building an empire,' she said softly. 'Proving his worth, over and over, to a mother who never loved him, an heiress who wouldn't believe in him, and a best friend who didn't support him.'

'That's not a fair call, Gabrielle.' Simone's voice was low and tight. 'It wasn't like that.'

'I know,' said Gabrielle. 'And on an intellectual level, Rafe would agree with you. He knows Luc's hands were tied when it came to setting up in business with him. He's quite capable of admitting that you and he were far too young to be thinking about marriage, let alone eloping to Australia. He *says* he works like a dog because he enjoys it. But if you ask me—and you did—the real reason he works so hard is that the ghosts from his childhood won't let him stop.'

'I think I need more wine,' said Simone.

Gabrielle held out her own champagne flute as Simone reached for the bottle. 'Hit me.'

'Don't tempt me,' muttered Simone as she refilled Gabrielle's glass and then her own. 'We probably shouldn't talk about brothers, you and me.'

'No, we probably shouldn't.' Gabrielle smiled faintly. 'By the way, I saw yours again today. I really thought I'd be able to handle it. Handle *him*. I couldn't.'

'I'm not surprised,' said Simone. 'I've yet to meet a woman who can. A word of advice, Gaby, from my heart to yours. Luc changed after you left. He grew up, grew tough, and got guarded. He's not an easy man to know.

Not an easy man to love. Believe me, plenty have tried.'

'Is that a warning?'

'More a plea to be careful,' said Simone. 'You used to be able to turn Luc's head with a glance and I doubt you've lost the knack. Getting him to lay down his heart is a different matter altogether. Just…be careful.'

Gabrielle played with the blades of grass beneath her fingertips. 'I didn't come back for him, Simone. I don't even know if I still want him. I haven't forgotten what came of wanting him before.'

'Neither has he,' murmured Simone. 'My advice was for if you were still interested in him. If you're not, then maybe all you need do is talk with him about what happened all those years ago and see if you can both put it behind you. Maybe that's the way to handle this.'

'You mean be civilised,' said Gabrielle. 'Me and Luc.'

Simone's lips twitched. 'Yes.'

'Civilised sounds wonderful,' said Gabrielle wistfully. 'Except for the dredging up the past bit. You don't suppose there's a way of being all civilised and restrained without bringing up the past at all?'

'Well, you could try,' said Simone thoughtfully. 'Why don't you come over to Caverness tomorrow afternoon and take a wander through the gardens with me? You could stay for a meal. Try again with Josien if you've a mind to, although I don't fully recommend it. You could attempt a civil discussion with Luc. See if you can find common ground that isn't rooted in the past. Ask his opinion on setting up a distribution arm here for your Australian reds. Make him feel useful. Men like that.'

'Then what?' said Gabrielle somewhat sceptically.

'Then you mention your fiancé.'

'I don't have a fiancé.'

'Not sure you need to mention that.' Simone started grinning and it wasn't because of the bubbles. 'All right, forget the non-existent fiancé. Set the boundaries for your relationship with Luc some other way—but set them nonetheless. Maybe Luc will follow your lead.'

'And if he doesn't?'

'Run,' said Simone, and kept right on grinning. 'Damn, I've missed you. Here's to hilltop reunions, restraint when dealing with troublesome men, and laying to rest the ghosts of our past.'

'Hear hear,' said Gabrielle and lifted her near-empty not-plastic champagne flute to her lips. Where had all the champagne gone? 'Restraint, you said?'

'Civilised restraint,' amended Simone. 'Nothing to it. More champagne?'

Gabrielle hesitated. 'Didn't you just fill my glass?'

'They're very little glasses,' said Simone sneakily. 'May I remind you we're talking Chateau Caverness 1955 here? This isn't just any old champagne.'

Indeed it wasn't. 'All right,' said Gabrielle, and reached for the magnum with what she thought was a great deal of restraint, never mind Simone's descent into helpless laughter. 'Maybe just one.'

CHAPTER THREE

AT FIVE pm the following afternoon, after an evening of laughter with Simone followed by half a day of sleep, Gabrielle drove, yet again, through the entrance to Chateau des Caverness and parked her car in the gravel courtyard next to the servants' quarters. Ignoring the door to her childhood completely, she switched on her mobile and found the number Simone had keyed into the phone last night.

'Where are you?' she said when Simone answered the phone.

'In the orchard, waiting for you,' said Simone. 'And if you've waited until now to tell me you're not coming I'm going to be very *very* annoyed.'

'I'm here,' said Gabrielle. 'I just didn't want to walk through three acres of garden looking for you, that's all. I'm not exactly wearing sensible shoes.'

'Colour me intrigued,' said Simone. 'I thought you'd be wearing something restrained.'

'I am wearing something restrained,' said Gabrielle. Her square necked knee-length plum-coloured sundress was very restrained. She'd even plaited her wayward hair and woven it into a heavy bun on top of her head, princess style, and secured it with a thousand pins. She'd followed up with the application of very subtle, very expensive, make-up and only the merest dash of her favourite perfume. She was a walking, talking picture of stylish restraint. 'Except for the shoes.'

The leather sandals with their delicate straps and flimsy heel were an exercise in idiocy. Idiocy being the word that summed up Gabrielle's thoughts on accepting Simone's invitation to tour the gardens and stay for dinner afterwards. Civilised restraint was all well and good in theory. Putting it into practice was hard.

'Take your shoes off, then, and come around the front way on the grass,' suggested Simone.

'That's not exactly civilised,' said Gabrielle. 'It's a little unrestrained.'

'Do it anyway,' said Simone with a snicker. 'Get all that wild abandon out of your system now so that when you happen across Luc there'll be none left for him.'

'You're making a surprising amount of sense,' muttered Gabrielle.

'I always do,' said Simone as Gabrielle reached the stone wall, slipped off her shoes, and stepped through the archway and into the formal front gardens. There'd been a box-hedge maze in here years ago. A maze that had towered high over her head and had provided endless hours of play for all the children of Caverness; her and Simone as well as Rafael and Luc. To Gabrielle's delight, the maze was still there, although these days it didn't tower over her but stood chest high so that a person could see the summer gazebo at its centre.

'You kept the maze,' she said into the phone.

'I kept the maze,' said Simone. 'You want to do this tour by phone or are you actually planning to converse face to face?'

'Picky picky,' murmured Gabrielle. 'I brought a few things for the dinner table. I'll put them on the terrace on the way round. See you soon.'

Sandals in one hand, goody bag in the other, Gabrielle skirted the maze and headed through the formal statuette garden towards the grand entrance to the chateau. Gabrielle's footsteps slowed when she saw that the terrace was already in use, but then she squared her shoulders and continued on her path. The grey stone steps were cool and hard beneath her feet after the softness and warmth of the summer grass, but she would not linger long, and she did not put her shoes on. 'Good afternoon, *Maman*, Hans,' she said to the seated pair. Gabrielle glanced warily at the third person to complete the tableau. Luc wasn't sitting and didn't look as if he had been sitting with the others. He looked as if he'd been simply passing by and had merely stopped for a word. 'Luc.'

Hans greeted her cheerfully. Josien's greeting was far more subdued but it *was* a greeting and Gabrielle felt pathetically grateful for it. Luc said nothing.

'I'm just on my way to meet up with Simone,' said Gabrielle, feeling intrusive and out of place. 'She's determined to give me a tour of the gardens.'

Josien's gaze flickered over Gabrielle, taking in her attire and her hair and the sandals hanging loosely from her fingertips, and Gabrielle smothered the impulse to check herself over for dirt and stains. Yes,

Gabrielle wanted to reconnect with her mother, but not if it meant becoming Josien's whipping girl again. This was who she was, the woman she'd grown up to be, and if Josien wasn't satisfied with her appearance or her behaviour then so be it. Gabrielle took a deep breath, set her shopping bag on the wire table beside her mother, and stood a little straighter. Luc still hadn't said a word. Okay, so their last meeting had been a little…tense, at times, and maybe he didn't want her here any more than Josien did, but would it have killed him to say hello? How was she supposed to act civilised if he wouldn't even afford her that small courtesy?

'Simone took the gardens in hand a few years back,' said Luc into an increasingly awkward silence. 'She's been focussing on the old orchard area of late. Most of the trees have gone to make way for roses. But not all.'

Gabrielle tucked an escapee strand of hair behind her ear with nervous fingers. Finally, a conversation. She could do conversation. Sort of. 'It sounds lovely.' She delved into her grocery bag and withdrew a posy of violets, their delicate scent filling the air as she set them carefully on the table. 'For you, *Maman*. I had planned to leave them with

Hans, but seeing as you're here…' Gabrielle turned to go before Josien could reject them to her face.

'Thank you.' Josien's reply came to her on the breeze, thready and formal but a reply nonetheless. Gabrielle looked back at her mother and Josien held her gaze but only for a moment before she looked away, her hands folded tightly in her lap. Luc looked stern. Hans was eyeing Josien curiously. With a heavy, deliberate tread Hans rose from his chair, crossed to the table and picked up the posy. 'My mother used to like violets too,' he said in his big gruff voice as he thrust them into Josien's hand. 'Pretty little things.'

Gabrielle didn't stick around to see the result. With the fear of rejection rising up inside her like a tidal wave, she fled.

Luc caught up with Gabrielle towards the bottom of the stairs leading down into the formal knot garden. 'Mind if I join you?' he said.

'No.' She glanced at him warily.

'You left your bag on the table,' he said next. 'I didn't know if you meant to or not. I left it there.'

She hadn't meant to. But there was no

going back for it now. 'I'll get it later.' When
Josien had gone. What had Simone suggested by way of civilised discussion again?
Gabrielle couldn't remember. Her brain was
too busy trying to deny the raw sexual appeal
of the man striding alongside her.

Yesterday Luc had been wearing working
attire—a suit befitting the head of the House
of Duvalier. Today his clothes ran to casual.
A blue shirt with a boldly embossed stripe
running through it—it was shaped to accen-
tuate the breadth of his shoulders and had
tiny tortoiseshell buttons all the way down
the front. The size of those buttons was more
in keeping with the size of a woman's fingers
than a man's and made Gabrielle's fingers
dance with wanting to free them from their
buttonholes. She ordered those wayward
fingers still and dragged her gaze away from
his chest and those buttons and concentrated
on the rest of him.

Big mistake.

Luc's trousers and work-roughened boots
were more suited to the fields than to the
boardroom, but they didn't look out of place
on him, not one little bit. All they did was
give his inherent sexuality a dangerously
earthy edge.

Luc could do mindless, earthy abandon just as easily as Gabrielle could. She knew it for a fact.

'How do you like living in Australia?' he asked her as they started walking through the formal French garden with its neatly clipped hedges. It was a question any acquaintance might ask her, new or old. A civilised question. A question that took her thoughts in a different direction altogether from the place they'd been headed.

Thank goodness.

'I like it fine,' she said and summoned a smile. 'Australia's a beautiful country. There's opportunity there. Less of a class system.' Her smile turned rueful. 'I wasn't the housekeeper's daughter once I reached Australia, I was the sophisticated French girl with the Australian father and a brother who'd just bought a beat-up old winery and renamed it Angels Landing. I could be whoever and whatever I wanted to be. I could be me. It was very liberating.'

'I can imagine,' murmured Luc with a swift white smile. 'Did you run wild?'

'Oddly enough, no.' Gabrielle swung her arm as they walked, setting her sandals to swinging like a lazy pendulum. 'Once there was nothing to rebel against I stopped rebelling.'

'I bet Rafe was relieved.'

'Maybe,' said Gabrielle. 'And maybe he always knew that as soon as I'd broken free of this place I would find my way.'

'You sound as if you hated it here,' said Luc.

'I didn't.' Gabrielle shook her head and looked around her at the chateau and the grounds surrounding it. 'I don't. How can you hate something so beautiful? No, it was my place in the grand scheme of things here that I hated. It wasn't that I necessarily wanted to own Caverness, you understand.' She didn't want Luc to think that. 'I just didn't want Caverness to own me.'

'I understand.' Luc's eyes had darkened. 'How do you feel about coming back here?'

'Conflicted,' said Gabrielle with brutal honesty. 'Part of me feels like I've come home. The rest of me's desperate to get away. I know there's no place for me here, Luc. Not in Josien's mind and probably not in yours or Simone's either, although you're both being very kind.'

'You're wrong,' said Luc. 'There's room for you here, Gabrielle. Always.'

'We'll see.'

'Gabrielle, if ever you need my help with anything, *ask*,' Luc said carefully. 'You'll get it.'

'Why?'

'You were driven from your home because of me.'

'The way I remember it,' said Gabrielle with a swift sideways glance for his stern profile, 'there were two of us in that grotto that night. Besides, I may have lost one home but I soon found another and found myself in the process. I know I fought against leaving here initially, Luc.' Gabrielle winced at the memory of the scene she'd caused— the pleading and the tears, the utter desolation that had enveloped her and that everyone, Luc included, had been witness to. 'But it helped me to grow up.' Grow up strong.

'And your estrangement from your mother?'

'Would probably have happened anyway,' said Gabrielle with a shrug. 'Lose the guilt, Luc. It doesn't suit you.'

Luc's eyes flashed fire. 'Careful, Gabrielle.'

'Much better,' she murmured. 'All that buttoned-down fire. That's very you.'

All that buttoned-down fire came roaring to the surface as Luc caught her by the arm and drew her into the secluded shadow of the chateau walls. He stood there, glaring at her in silence as he let the awareness between them build. And build. 'Why do you *do* that?' he said at last. 'You push and you push and then you push me some more. I warn you, but you never seem to *listen*.'

'I'm listening now,' she said through suddenly dry lips, and took a step backwards only to come up against solid stone wall. 'I'm listening very intently.'

'Good, because I'm choosing my words carefully. Do you remember how it was when I lost control with you, Gabrielle? Do you? Is that what you want from me?'

'No.'

Yes, said a little voice that would not be silenced.

'No,' she said more firmly. 'I want us to be civil with one another. That's all.'

'Civil,' he said mirthlessly. 'Around you?'

'Yes.'

'God help me.'

'You could at least *try*,' she said darkly. 'You can't even greet me properly.'

'Have you ever stopped to wonder *why*?' he grated.

She hadn't. All she'd seen was the lack of what he bestowed on others so naturally.

'Just remember, this was your idea, not mine,' he muttered, his voice a dark delicious rumble as he set his palms to the stone wall either side of her and bent his head to hers. 'You want my greeting, here it is. *Bonjour*, Gabrielle.' She felt the fleeting warmth of his lips against her cheek and then his lips were gone. The heat in her cheek started to spread. Probably best to ignore it. She pulled back ever so slightly to find him staring down at her, his expression thunderous. 'See?' she said tentatively. 'That wasn't so bad.'

'I haven't finished yet,' he murmured, and set his lips to her other cheek. He started higher on her cheekbone this time, and lingered longer, tracing a meandering path along her cheek to her mouth where he very discreetly, very deliberately, wet the corner of her mouth with his tongue.

Gabrielle gasped, she couldn't help it, as an answering burn started low in her stomach.

'Say *"Bonjour, Lucien"*,' he whispered, his lips barely leaving hers. Say *"Comment ça va?"* and try to stop your body from aching because you want to feel more of me.

Clench your hands into fists all you like, angel, but sooner or later someone's going to figure out that you're not angry, you're just aroused. Under normal circumstances there'd be people around us, watching us, waiting to see what takes place between us. Do you really want them to see what happens next, Gabrielle? Do you?'

'No,' she whispered. 'This isn't going to be civilised, is it?'

Luc smiled briefly. 'No.' And brushed his lips against hers with the lightest pressure, the faintest whisper of heat, but it was enough to make Gabrielle close her eyes and tilt her head the better to receive more of him. He settled his lips against hers more firmly and his hand came up to cup her face, cool fingers on heated cheeks before he slid his thumb to her jawbone and his fingers into her hair. His mouth moved over hers, still civilised, but only just. This wasn't a simple kiss of greeting, nothing like it. There was a question in this kiss. And for Gabrielle there had only ever been one answer. With a shuddering sigh, Gabrielle opened her mouth and let him in.

Luc knew that kissing Gabrielle was a mistake; he'd always known. She held nothing back, she never had, as she opened for him and spun them into oblivion, the kiss sliding from barely contained to outrageously wanton in a heartbeat. Her taste assaulted his senses, rich and heady, like the finest of wine. Her scent was one he would never tire of, not if he lived to be a hundred, and as for her touch... He wanted her hands on him more than he wanted to breathe.

'Touch me,' he murmured, between more of those greedy, soul-shattering kisses. 'For pity's sake, Gabrielle, touch me.'

With a ragged little noise, half sob, half plea, Gabrielle dropped her sandals, wound her arms around his neck and did as she was told.

The rain came suddenly, hitting hard, dousing them both with cool and stinging droplets. Gabrielle broke their kiss and gasped, flinching away, her arm coming up to protect her face from the spray. Luc blinked and shook his head before he too raised his hand to ward off the unexpected assault that didn't appear to be coming from overhead. 'What the hell..?'

'Sorry.' Simone's voice came to him as if from a great distance, never mind that she stood only a few feet away with a hose in her hand and an angelic expression on her face. 'I turned the tap on and the water pressure just whipped that hose right out of my hands and sprayed everything in sight. I simply couldn't control it.' Simone's level gaze pinned them both. 'You know how it is.'

Gabrielle blushed a fetching shade of pink.

Luc wiped the water from his face with his sleeve and rammed his hands in his pockets to stop them from reaching for Gabrielle again. 'Next time we meet in public I'm saying hello and that's *it*,' he told Gabrielle grimly.

'Good idea,' she murmured as she knelt down to pick up her sandals, the action putting her at eye level with certain parts of his anatomy still straining for attention. Luc looked away fast, clenching his jaw as he fixed his gaze upon the stone wall straight in front of him and kept it there.

'And then I'm heading for the other side of the room,' he told no one in particular, his gaze still firmly fixed on the wall. 'Possibly the other side of the earth.'

'It's called Australia,' said Simone dryly. 'And it certainly worked for the pair of you last time. More water?'

'No,' he said quickly.

'I'm good too.' Gabrielle popped into Luc's frame of view with the speed of a rain-drenched weed. She smiled brightly and shook out the droplets of water from her dress for good measure. 'So where were we?'

'About to take a tour of the gardens?' said Simone with the lift of an elegant eyebrow. 'Are you planning on joining us, brother?'

Not if he could possibly help it.

'Leave me alone with this woman and you're a dead man,' murmured Gabrielle.

'She'll get you alone sooner or later,' argued Luc. 'Why delay the inevitable?'

'Nothing's inevitable. Except maybe you and I needing to get that out of our system.' Gabrielle swept past him. 'At least it's done now. Finished. Lesson learned. No need for a repeat. Are you listening?'

'Intently,' he said dryly. 'You seriously believe we can just carry on being all civilised after that?'

'Absolutely.' Chin high, she headed for the nearest garden path and started to lead the way up it. 'I'm an extremely civilised person.'

'I noticed that,' said Simone, with a heartily amused grin as she sent Luc a wink and followed in Gabrielle's wake. 'So much fuss over such an ordinary little kiss. Really,

Luc. Take Gabrielle's lead and forget all about it. Put all that pesky kissing business far, far behind you. There are far more important things to consider on a day like today.'

'Like what?' What could be more important than contemplating the loss of one's control and quite possibly one's mind? And when he might conceivably have the opportunity to lose them again?

'Gardens,' said Simone firmly. 'Gardens are far more important than kisses—wouldn't you agree, Gabrielle?'

Gabrielle did agree. Heartily.

Women.

CHAPTER FOUR

DINNER that evening would have been both pleasant and relaxing, thought Gabrielle with a heartfelt glare in Simone's direction—if Luc hadn't decided to join them. She vaguely remembered ordering Luc not to leave her alone with his sister. She dimly recalled mentioning red-wine and hearing Simone talk of preparing a meal to accompany a red wine experience, but nowhere during the conversations that had taken place did she recall either her or Simone actually issuing Luc a dinner invitation. Not that he needed one, she decided glumly. Caverness being his home, and all.

It was just that, now that she had her wits about her, sharing a cosy home-cooked meal with Simone and Luc didn't seem like a very good idea at all. If she had any sense at all, she would stay as far away from Luc as she possibly could, the reason being that if he wasn't in sight she wouldn't want and if she didn't want she wouldn't touch. If she never touched, she would not take—and she would not lose herself in the process. Simple.

Problem solved.

The more immediate problem being how to make her exit without insulting her hosts. Simone would understand, surely.

'This civilised dinner thing—it really isn't working for me,' she said as Simone scooped stuffing mixture into the duck and plugged the hole shut with a parboiled and well-skewered orange.

'I'm pretty sure it's not working for the duck either,' murmured Simone, 'but do you see me stopping?' Simone swiftly began to squeeze the juice from two more oranges. 'It's your own fault. You shouldn't have mentioned that you'd brought two of Rafael's wines along. You should have known there'd be no getting rid of Luc after that.'

'My fault?' spluttered Gabrielle. '*My* fault? Who was it that promised him roast duck in citrus?' Or, in this particular case, citrus in roast duck. Duck had been Luc's favourite dish as a boy, and if the light in his eyes at its mention was anything to go by it was still a firm favourite. 'You deliberately planned to prepare something he couldn't resist.'

'Of course I did.' Simone was unrepentant. 'It's all part of the be-civil-to-Luc plan that we put together last night, remember? The fact that you couldn't manage to make that plan *stick* for more than two minutes in each other's company is hardly my fault.'

The fact that Simone was *right* was hardly reassuring.

'If you run out on this meal I'm going to be very displeased,' said Simone, fixing her with a stern glare. 'You can leave when the meal is over, not before.'

In which case it was time to move this meal along, decided Gabrielle as she surveyed the restaurant sized cooking bench currently strewn with ingredients. 'How can I help? Give me something to do.'

'Open the wine,' said Simone with a grin. 'That might help.'

'Luc's opening the wine.' Gabrielle slid a sideways glance to where he stood on the far side of the kitchen. 'Correction, he's examining the label at the moment.' Gabrielle felt a flutter of apprehension. The branding and labelling of the wine was her department, her work, and she took a great deal of pride in it. The Angels Landing label with its winged angel graphic and elegant raised text had won numerous industry awards in Australia but Australia wasn't France. Would her work find favour with Luc?

He looked up and caught her gaze. 'Bold,' he said.

'So's the wine.' Gabrielle tried to stop feeling protective of the product but to no avail. Years of work and a great deal of heart had gone into the making and presentation of that wine—she could never be blasé about people's reaction to it.

As winemakers themselves, Luc and Simone would understand.

'Go,' said Simone, nodding towards Luc and the wine, and Gabrielle headed swiftly across the kitchen, making sure to stay on the opposite side of the table to Luc.

'You wish to talk me through the tasting?' said Luc.

'If you'd like me to?' She'd tried for nonchalance, but if the tilt to Luc's lips was any indication she hadn't quite nailed it.

'I would,' he said with admirable formality. '*Merci.*' His smile widened. 'You always were good at selling wines to customers. Do you remember when you and Simone took over cellar door sales the afternoon Marciel fell ill? How many cases of our oldest and most expensive vintage did you sell? Twenty-eight?'

'Twenty-nine,' said Gabrielle. 'And we had a definite cuteness advantage over Marciel.' Marciel had been grey, grizzled, and formidable. She and Simone had been grubby, pinafored, and seven and nine years old respectively. Simone had been lauded for her efforts. Gabrielle felt her smile begin to falter as the memory returned in full. Gabrielle had been beaten for overstepping her boundaries.

With a horsewhip.

Rafe had gone ballistic when he'd seen the welts on her back and legs. He'd been thirteen and her champion but there'd been no protecting her from Josien. Not back then. Not until later, when Rafe's size, his strength, and his own icy fury at Josien's punishments had compelled Josien to think twice before meting them out.

'What is it?' asked Luc, his deep delicious voice reaching into her and dragging her back to the present. He always had been able to read her. It had been one of the best things about their friendship as children, and one of the dangers of being with him as she'd grown older and her crush on him had intensified. 'Gabrielle? What's wrong?'

'Nothing,' she said, deliberately letting go of unhappy memories and pasting on a smile. As children she and Rafe had been extremely adept at hiding Josien's cruelties from the world and she had no mind to expose them now. Some might call that weak, some might call her complicit in her own punishment, but to Gabrielle's way of thinking the word that should be used in those types of situations was *survivor*. She and Rafael were survivors both. And quietly, rightfully, proud of it. 'That one's our most mature wine,' she said, indicating the bottle in Luc's hand. 'Having said that, it's still only five years old. Rafe wanted to give it another year before releasing it, but economics got in the way. We needed the cash flow,' she said. 'This wine is one year younger and we've only bottled a small amount of it. Most of the vintage is still in barrels,' she said indicating the bottle on the counter. 'They're both beautifully balanced wines, don't get me wrong, but the younger one's my favourite. It's my favourite out of all the wines we've produced to date.'

'Why red wine?' asked Luc. 'Why didn't Rafe stick with what he knew? He took with him a lot of knowledge about the making of sparkling wine.'

Indeed he had. Both Luc and Rafe had learned a great deal from old man Duvalier about the making of champagne. Luc had been a skilled practitioner even then. In contrast, Rafe had been inclined to experiment. Most of Rafe's experiments had failed but sometimes…sometimes his wild combinations had garnered even old man Duvalier's praise. 'I don't know why he went for the reds, in all honesty,' said Gabrielle. 'He'd just bought the vineyard when I arrived on his doorstep. As far as I can gather he saw that old winery and fell in love. The vines in the ground were red varieties so red was the wine he made.'

'Why the Angels Landing name?' asked Luc.

'Because it fit,' said Gabrielle with a tiny half smile. Because Angels Tears hadn't exactly cut muster as an uplifting name for a new beginning. No need to mention that she'd labelled Rafe's first bottling of a barrel of private stock Angels Tears, or that it was the best of Rafe's reds by far. It wasn't for public consumption, not the name and not the wine. 'Open them.' Never mind that they wouldn't get through both, Luc would want to compare vintages.

'What made you go for corks instead of a screw top?' asked Luc as he obliged.

'Tradition,' said Gabrielle. 'Rafe knows exactly which market he's targeting and they don't do screw tops. Yet.'

Bottles opened and wine breathing, Luc took his time collecting glassware from the cupboard while Gabrielle watched him with a combination of exasperation, lust, and a growing knot of trepidation. Luc's opinion of the wine mattered to her. If he didn't like it she was going to be crushed.

'Colour's good,' murmured Luc after pouring three tasting serves from the first bottle.

'Yes.' The colour was superb. She waited for Luc to pick up his glass and willed herself not to fidget. 'Simone, do you want some?'

Simone's face was a study in contradiction as she headed almost reluctantly towards them. 'I'd feel a lot better about this if I could separate the maker from his wine,' she muttered.

'I'd feel a lot better if we could just get this over with,' countered Gabrielle. 'Just try some and be done with it. Say hmm, quite nice, very interesting, and put me out of my misery.'

But that wasn't the way wine tasting worked at Chateau des Caverness.

'Bouquet's a little…' began Luc with his nose to the glass.

'A little what?' asked Gabrielle anxiously.

'Interesting,' said Luc. Was he smirking? She couldn't see his mouth for the wine glass but his eyes were definitely laughing at her.

'Nice berry notes,' said Simone.

'Apricot as well,' said Luc. 'Unusual. Hmm.'

'For heaven's sake, Luc, will you get to the "quite nice" part?' muttered Gabrielle.

Luc smiled, briefly, and his eyes took on a rakish gleam. 'Patience, angel,' he murmured. 'Wine tasting's a civilised business. I thought you knew that. Being such a civilised and re-strained person yourself and all.'

She usually was. Around anyone but him. 'Luc,' she said with what she considered a great deal of restraint, 'don't make me hurt you.' Gabrielle took a calming breath and turned her attention to the irregular streaks running through the marble bench-top—like little rivers and estuaries they meandered and widened, separated and petered out. She wished her awareness of this man would peter out too, but the more time she spent in Luc's company, the stronger it grew. She wanted to know what he thought of her wine. She wanted to know what he thought of their recent kiss. And heaven help her but she wanted to kiss him again. What would happen if she and Luc did embark on an affair? A steamy, searing, no-holds-barred exercise in raunch? Would that be enough to get him out of her system? Would it leave her sated and ready to move on or would spending time in Luc's embrace spoil her for all other men?

She really didn't like the sound of that last option at all. No. No, thank you. No.

'What are you thinking?' murmured Luc.

Gabrielle glanced up and sent him a careful smile. 'Nothing that concerns you.' She waited some more while the ever so civilised head of the House of Duvalier faffed about with his wine. 'Well?' she said impatiently. 'Can we skip to the civilised part now?'

'Well, I like it,' said Simone. 'It's a big-bodied and very bold wine with a depth and smoothness that belies its age.' Simone smiled briefly and took another sip. 'I don't know what it is about these Australian wines… there's always such richness of *flavour*.'

'Rafe thinks it's a reflection of the youth of the wine industry there,' said Gabrielle.

'Everyone's still experimenting. There hasn't been time to develop a whole lot of ritual or subtlety.'

'There's subtlety here,' said Luc, tasting the wine and lifting his glass to once more study the colour.

'You think so?' Gabrielle let her pleasure at his words seep through her. 'I think so too. Try the other bottle.'

Luc tasted the second one and his smile turned wry. 'The last one had some excellent qualities embedded in it,' he said. 'This one's brilliant.'

Simone sighed. Gabrielle beamed.

'What kind of distribution are you aiming for?' asked Luc, his eyes sharp and his words all business. Gabrielle hadn't seen this side of him before. She liked it. Liked that he took her expansion plans seriously.

'The exclusive kind,' she said. 'We're not looking to inundate the market. We just want to establish a presence here.'

'What do you need?'

'Storage, for starters.'

'In the caves?'

'Preferably, yes.'

'You'll pay premium price for that.'

'I know.' Gabrielle sighed. 'And, realistically speaking, underground storage may not be feasible hereabouts. I'm looking into all the options on offer.'

'What else do you need?'

'A marketing development strategy, a workable entry-level price point, and an on-ground sales force.'

'Who do you have in place for those?'

'Me.' Luc would have had an entire team working on it, but she didn't have those kinds of resources. She waited for him to say that it couldn't be done, she waited for his lips to curve in an indulgent smile as he humoured the bit player, but he didn't do either of those things.

'Busy times, these next few weeks,' he said.

'Yes.'

'Let me know if you need an introduction to some of the major distributors in the area,' he said next. 'I'll set something up for you. A tasting, perhaps. You could use the facilities already in place at Caverness. That might work.'

Gabrielle tried to keep her mouth closed, never mind that it wanted to drop open. A Chateau des Caverness wine-tasting session was an experience savoured by even the most jaded industry stalwarts and it wasn't just because of the quality of the product. Stepping into the cellars behind the chateau was like stepping into history. There were caverns filled with vintage champagne. Tiny grottos with tea light candles sitting in scooped-out hollows in the walls. Pyramids of bottled wine stacked in carved-out triangles in those same cave walls. Rough-hewn tables set ready for impromptu wine tasting. Narrow passageways flanked by rusty iron gates, cave paintings that dated back centuries, and always the cool grey rock beneath the fingertips. Sensual and seductive, the caves of Caverness existed to woo the senses of *extremely* discerning buyers.

'Of course, if I'm going to put the House of Duvalier's reputation on the line I'll need to know a little more about your production schedule and what sized contracts you're capable of fulfilling.'

Luc the businessman.

And what on earth was the businesswoman Gabrielle going to say in reply? Luc's offer was a generous one and completely unexpected—the patronage of the House of Duvalier would go a long way towards securing orders from exactly the type of buyers she and Rafael hoped to target. She *should* be jumping all over the idea.

She wasn't.

Rafe wouldn't like it. He wouldn't want that kind of connection to Simone. For her part, Gabrielle didn't particularly want to do business with Luc. Her feelings for Luc were complicated enough. Tying the growth of one's business to the goodwill of a man she'd just been contemplating having a passionate and potentially short-lived affair with didn't seem like a particularly sensible idea.

'You can talk to me about that,' she said guardedly. 'Better still, why don't I talk to Rafe and get back to you? You might not need to know about production schedules and estimates of vintage sizes at all.'

'You don't think he'd go for the idea?' asked Luc.

'I don't know what he'd think,' said Gabrielle. 'Rafe's not one for accepting charity. Or for becoming indebted to people.' She was back to choosing her words carefully. 'It's a generous offer, Lucien, and I thank you for it. But I just don't know if we can accept it.' She smiled a little wryly. 'Your father would turn in his grave.'

'My father, for all his good points—and,

yes, he did have some—was an extremely short-sighted man. He should have backed Rafe when he had the chance.'

But he hadn't. The words lay there in the silence, all the more potent for remaining unsaid.

'I'll phone Rafe and put the notion to him,' said Luc. And at Gabrielle's open-mouthed astonishment, 'What?'

'You don't think a mediator might come in handy?' said Gabrielle. 'I mean, you haven't spoken to him in seven years and now all of a sudden this?'

'What makes you think I haven't phoned him in seven years?' asked Luc curiously.

'I, ah… Have you?'

'Many times,' he said, and at Gabrielle's continued shock, 'Which bit surprises you most? That Rafe and I have kept in contact or that you didn't know about it?'

'Both,' she admitted baldly. Rafael had been so disillusioned when he'd left for Australia. Gabrielle hadn't thought he'd kept in contact with *anyone* from Caverness. Not Lucien, not Josien, and certainly not Simone. 'What do you talk about?'

This time it was Luc's turn to look wary. 'Everything but sisters.'

* * *

As far as exquisite food and fabulous surroundings were concerned, the meal was a
resounding success. By mutual, unspoken
agreement they'd stripped the conversation
of anything remotely concerning the past
once they'd settled down to eat, concentrating instead on the present and the future.
Simone expanded on her plans for the
garden. Luc spoke of the experimental champagne varieties he hoped to trial once he
acquired more land. They spoke of the
changes that had taken place in the village
over the last few years. The new priest, the
newly formed men's choir. The opera diva
who'd purchased a crumbling chateau for a
song and had kept the local tradesmen in
work for years in her effort to restore it to its
former glory. Her pockets were deep, according to Lucien. Her youthful face was a testi-
mony to the marvels of modern surgical
techniques, according to Simone. She'd had
widowed heads of dynastic champagne
houses falling over their feet to court her.

She'd just silenced gossiping tongues completely by marrying a local widowed thatcher
some ten years her junior, who came
complete with thinning hair, three little ones
in tow, not two euros to his name, and a

heart—according to the villagers in the know—of pure gold.

'But doesn't that make her outcast amongst the upper echelons of society here?' asked Gabrielle, fascinated. 'And what do *his* friends think of *her*? Where do they fit?'

'According to them, together,' said Simone. 'The village is slowly coming to terms with it.'

Gabrielle grinned. 'Good for them.'

'The villagers or the happy couple?' asked Luc dryly.

'Both.'

'The village is changing,' said Simone. 'There's new blood in it, a younger generation with fewer ties to the old ways. It's not as class conscious.'

Gabrielle eyed Simone curiously. 'I'm not saying you're wrong,' she said. 'But, Simone, every door has always been open to you. How do you know it's not as class conscious? People knew who I was the minute I stepped in the village. Knew I was Josien's daughter and judged me accordingly. I didn't think much had changed at all.'

'How did they judge you?' asked Luc, his eyes sharp.

'When I asked for a room I was offered the

smallest and cheapest. Servant class all the way,' she said with a tight smile. 'I was too tired to argue.'

Luc's lips tightened. 'Stay here, then.'

Gabrielle shook her head. 'I was not too tired to argue today. I've moved into a bigger suite with its own bathroom facilities. Madame very curtly implied that this was doubtless a luxury I wasn't used to and asked for the entire three weeks' payment in advance. In cash.'

'Old bat,' said Simone. 'I never did like that woman. What did you do?'

'I gave her a week's worth and told her I'd keep an eye out for something more spacious.'

'Caverness is spacious,' said Luc darkly. 'Very spacious.'

'To buy,' said Gabrielle.

'Wish I'd been there to see the look on her face when you said you were looking to buy,' said Simone.

'You wish to *buy* property hereabouts?' barked Luc.

'It's your lucky day,' murmured Gabrielle to Simone. 'You get to witness the look on Luc's face instead. It's equally incredulous.'

'It's not incredulous,' snapped Luc, shutting his astonishment down fast. 'You took me by surprise, that's all. Given your conflicted feelings about returning to these parts I'd have thought acquiring property here a reckless move.'

Rafe thought the same. Not that Gabrielle felt inclined to mention it. 'I guess we'll all just have to wait and see,' she said.

'Have you looked at the old Hammer-schmidt place yet, like I told you to?' asked Simone.

'Not yet.'

'This isn't incredulity on my face,' said Luc tightly. 'No, wait. Yes, it is. But it's not for you or your possible ability to afford such a purchase,' he told Gabrielle before turning to glare at his sister. 'It's for *her*.'

'Don't you look all snarly at me,' said Simone. 'You want the land but don't know what to do with the rest of it. Gabrielle needs storage and distribution facilities and some-where to live. Hmm, let me think.' Simone put her fingers to her temples and closed her eyes. 'I'm sensing a mutually beneficial solution here.'

'No,' said Luc.

'No,' echoed Gabrielle. 'Not going to happen, Simone. Luc's not looking for a part-nership arrangement and neither am I.'

'Just a suggestion,' murmured Simone.

'Yes, well, it's not one of your better ones,' said Gabrielle with dark amusement. 'You could always telephone Rafael and suggest *you* buy the vineyard in partnership with *him*,' she suggested sweetly. 'You've doubtless kept in regular contact with him all these years as well.'

'Wrong,' said Simone. 'I'm as much of a stranger to the let's-part-as-friends concept as you are. Can we change the subject now?'

'With pleasure,' said Luc and reached for his wine.

CHAPTER FIVE

GABRIELLE did not linger over after-dinner coffee. She drank the brew down hot and black, helped Simone and Luc sort the kitchen, gathered her scattered belongings together on the kitchen bench and excused herself to make use of the powder room before she left for the village.

Gabrielle did not need to be told where the nearest bathroom was. It was along the great hallway, turn right, past the stairs, first door on the right. She didn't notice Josien standing at the bottom of the stairs until she drew level with her. So still, thought Gabrielle with more than a flicker of apprehension. So still and silent, like a statue—a cold and beautiful marble statue. *'Maman.'* Had Josien been waiting for her? Hans had informed them earlier that Josien had retired to her suite. According to Simone, that was

Josien's usual practice and in no way connected to Gabrielle's presence at the dinner table. Forget her, Simone had directed, and Gabrielle had for the most part succeeded in doing just that. 'I— Hi.' She tried a tentative smile. 'Did you wish to see me?'

'I suppose you think you're one of them now,' said Josien bleakly. 'Socialising with them, inviting yourself to dine with them.'

Gabrielle felt her smile falter.

'You never did know your place.'

'On the contrary, *Maman*, you never let me forget it.' Gabrielle drew herself upright, determined not to be Josien's whipping girl—not this time. Not ever again. 'But you are right in one respect. I'm no longer bound by your version of where I belong. This time *I* decide where I fit into the fabric of society here, not you. And if I want to have a meal with my childhood friends, I will.'

'He'll never marry you, you know.' Her mother's beautiful face was so at odds with the ugliness of her words. 'You're not in his league.'

Gabrielle could think of only one man her mother could be talking about. 'Maybe I don't want to marry him, *Maman*. Have you ever considered that possibility?'

'Then why did you come back? Flaunting your precious vineyard and your fancy clothes. Do you really think a little bit of wealth will make the slightest difference to a man like Lucien? You're still the housekeeper's daughter, Gabrielle.'

'You underestimate me, *Maman*. You always have. And just for the record, I didn't come back for Lucien, I came back for you. That was a mistake. I see that now.'

'Where did Rafael get the money to buy the vineyard?' asked Josien, her abrupt change of topic causing Gabrielle to blink in her effort to keep up with the conversation, if you could call it that. 'Who staked him?'

'Harrison,' said Gabrielle. The father she'd only ever exchanged birthday and Christmas cards with until she'd joined Rafe in exile. The one who lived in Australia. The man whose name both Gabrielle and Rafael bore. 'Harrison Alexander. Remember him? The man you married? The man whose children you had? Rafe looked him up. You were wrong about him not wanting us, *Maman*. He did want us.'

'Harrison staked him?' Josien's voice trembled slightly. 'But why?'

'Maybe that's what fathers *do*,' said

Gabrielle wearily. She really didn't want to talk with Josien any more. Not about this. Not about anything. 'Why can't you just accept that Rafael finally found someone who believed in him, *Maman*? Why must you taint everything with sourness and disbelief?'

Josien stayed silent.

'I'm going to the washroom,' Gabrielle told her mother. 'And then I'm heading back to the village. Don't feel you have to wait around for me to leave. I know my own way out.'

Josien turned, her chin high and that exquisite face thrown into perfect relief. Gabrielle knew that face. Loved it. Despaired of it.

'He always was soft, Harrison.' Josien's words came to her as a whisper; Gabrielle wasn't even sure her mother had meant for her to hear them. 'Too soft for the likes of me. I should never have married him but I was desperate, you see. Desperate to escape this place, desperate to be someone I wasn't, and Harrison was in love with me, in love with my face. He didn't see what was underneath until it was too late. I never let him see.' Josien turned to stare at Gabrielle and the desolation in her eyes almost swallowed

Gabrielle whole. 'Harrison Alexander may be your father, Gabrielle, but he's not Rafael's.' She turned and began her ascent up the stairs, leaning heavily on the handrail for support. 'And he knows it.'

'No,' whispered Gabrielle. Caring and supportive, Harrison had always been there for her and Rafael these past seven years. They would never have achieved what they'd achieved without his unwavering support and encouragement. 'I don't believe you.' And when her mother continued wordlessly, regally, up the stairs, leaving Gabrielle staring up at her from below with white-knuckled fists and hot and prickling eyes, 'You're lying!'

Luc Duvalier was a success story by anyone's standards. He had it all. Wealth. Health. Family. And youth. He was twenty-nine. He ran a Champagne dynasty that was the envy of his peers, brokered multimillion-euro deals with monotonous regularity, and had a reputation for being relaxed and in control no matter what the situation.

He'd never worked harder at being relaxed and in control than he'd worked tonight. He'd succeeded though. Gabrielle had eventually settled down and he'd almost managed to forget the kiss they'd shared earlier, aided somewhat by Simone's expertise as a hostess and the delivery of his favourite food. All he had to do now was see Gabrielle to her car without forfeiting the tentative trust he'd built with her over the past few hours and the evening would be, by anyone's standards, a resounding success. Civilised even, though he was loath to bandy the word about too soon.

Simone had disappeared, to put the garbage out, even though Luc had offered to do it.

'This is the part where you show Gabrielle that you can be trusted alone with her at the end of an evening,' Simone had told him in a deceptively gentle voice. 'I have faith in you,' she'd added, only this time her voice had held an underlying hint of steel that he'd recognised of old. He wasn't the only Duvalier around here who liked things neat and tidy and right.

And then Gabrielle walked back into the kitchen white-faced, and eyes bright with what looked a lot like unshed tears. She tried on a smile but it was a dismal effort and one she soon abandoned. 'Time to go,' she murmured and collected her belongings from the table with trembling hands. 'Where's Simone?'

'Outside. She'll be back soon.'

Gabrielle moved jerkily towards the kitchen door. 'I'll catch her on my way out. Thank you, Lucien, for the pleasant evening.' She hesitated, before reluctantly holding out her hand as if expecting him to shake it. He didn't touch her, he didn't dare.

'What's wrong?' he said curtly.

'Nothing.' She withdrew her hand, clutching at her handbag as if it held crown jewels.

'I won't touch you, if that's what's bothering you,' he said. 'I can be civil around you, Gabrielle. I have been.'

'I know.' She looked stricken. Correction, even more stricken, if that was possible. 'I've enjoyed your company, Lucien. I really have. As for our kiss, well…I enjoyed that too,' she said baldly. 'Possibly a little too much. I'm all for ignoring it and hoping the impulse to kiss you some more will go away.'

'It's been seven years, Gabrielle,' he said grimly. 'And it hasn't gone away.'

'Or we could stay away from one another. Cut and run,' she said with another smile that didn't reach her eyes. 'I'm all in favour of that particular approach. It's tried and true. Proven.'

'We could explore it,' he said. Another option, and one he wanted on the table. 'You and me. And this. You're not sixteen any more, Gabrielle. And I'm not honour-bound to stay away from you. There's nothing stopping us from exploring the attraction between us.'

'No.' Her eyes darkened. Pain flashed through them again. What the hell was wrong with her? 'No, I suppose not.'

'So I'll call you,' he said. 'About setting up that wine tasting.'

'Yes.'

'Or you call me. Tomorrow some time. About meeting for dinner again soon.'

'Yes.'

Unease settled over him. She was telling him what he wanted to hear. Telling him whatever he wanted to hear in order to get away from him, unless he missed his guess. While her eyes telegraphed panic and no small measure of pain. 'Gabrielle, what's wrong? What happened between here and the powder room?'

'Nothing. Really, Luc. It's nothing. You've been a gentleman all evening.' She found a brilliant smile from somewhere and pasted it on her lips. 'A rakish and charming gentleman and I've thoroughly enjoyed you. I'm just not ready to risk a goodnight kiss with you without a garden hose handy, that's all.'

He let her walk to the door on that remark, let her turn the handle and turn her head and glance at him through eyes that told him that there was something else going on here. Something he didn't understand. But he let her go, let her take refuge in humour. If she wouldn't confide in him there was nothing else he could do.

'Goodnight, Gabrielle,' he murmured wryly. 'Sweet dreams, and just for the record… I'm not ready to risk kissing you goodnight at all.'

Luc waited until he heard Simone's voice and Gabrielle's answering murmur before heading for the main hall and the powder room, scanning the tops of the sideboards and flower stands along the way for something, anything, that would have caused Gabrielle to become upset. He stood at the bottom of the grand staircase, and looked around again, puzzled. There was nothing here, nothing he could see that would have caused such a reaction from Gabrielle. Household trinkets. Vases. A painting of an ancestor or ten. That was all. He looked towards the top of the staircase thoughtfully. Had she gone upstairs?

Had someone else come down?

The only other two people staying in the chateau were Hans and Josien and they'd both retired for the evening long ago. Hadn't they?

He stood there, listening for the sound of Gabrielle's car engine starting, listening to the crunch of car tyres on loose courtyard gravel as she manoeuvred the vehicle carefully through the archway and accelerated down the drive. The kitchen door thudded shut and the sound of rapid footsteps on floorboards met his ears as he stood there in the hallway, in the half-light of a nearby lamp. That would be Simone.

No footsteps sounded overhead. No sound came from upstairs at all…except… He heard it then, a creak, slow and careful, and following on from it the soft metal click that went with the closing of a door.

Gabrielle fretted her way through the following day. The memory of Luc's most recent kiss tugged at her senses and the thought of his offer of dinner, not to mention his offer to let her use the caves of Caverness for a wine tasting for the Angels Landing reds, echoed through her brain. She needed to pay attention to such things. It was important to know where she was heading with regards to Luc for he was a force no sensible woman ignored, but Luc wasn't the only man on her mind today. Rafe had been on her mind too. Rafe, and everything else that went with Josien's declaration that Harrison wasn't his father. For the first time in her life, Gabrielle dreaded the thought of phoning her brother. Her stomach churned whenever she passed by the phone, eating away at her, making her feel ill. She hadn't asked for this secret. She wished to hell she didn't have to keep it. Rafe was her rock, the one constant in her life, and she hated to think that by keeping this information from him, she was betraying him.

But she hated the thought of damaging the relationship Rafe had with Harrison more.

Gabrielle cursed and slammed the door hard on thoughts of fathers who weren't fathers and the things she now knew that Rafael did not.

Poisonous words designed to destroy a relationship between father and son.

Weight-ridden words designed to build a chasm between sister and brother.

Cruel, loveless words from a mother who did not deserve the title.

Words she was not inclined to share with anyone. Not with Luc when he'd asked her what was wrong, and definitely not with Rafael. No, better to forget she'd ever heard those particular words and speak to Rafe of other matters altogether. Matters that would bring their own ghosts of the past along for the ride, and for once in her life she did not dread their reappearance. There were worse ghosts to fear and always had been.

She just hadn't known of them.

Who? Who could be Rafe's father? Not Phillipe Duvalier. Heaven help all of them and especially Rafe and Simone, but, please God, not him. There had been a slight partiality for Rafe on Phillipe's part. He'd encouraged Rafe's friendship with Luc. He'd made a creditable attempt at training Rafe in the business of winemaking once Rafe had shown an interest. He'd shown Rafe kindness, at times, but the kindness of a father? No.

Rafe didn't resemble the Duvaliers in looks. There was nothing of Josien's looks about him either, except perhaps in the perfection of facial features, albeit a more strongly hewn version. Rafe had Harrison's colouring. Fair hair and blue eyes. Bluer than Harrison's. Bluer and deeper.

Who if not Phillipe Duvalier?

Who if not Harrison?

'Doesn't matter,' Gabrielle told herself fiercely. 'Don't care.' And following swiftly on the heels of that declaration, *'How I hate her.'*

Such an unbridled, uncivilised emotion, hate, but this time, *this* time, she refused to push it away. With another heartfelt curse, she reached for the phone.

Rafe had a habit of barking out his name into the phone and following up with a brusque hello. This time was no exception.

'Is now a good time to call?' she asked him.

'Gabrielle?' Warmth crept into his voice like sunshine seeping through clouds on a stormy day. 'It's about time you called. I've just been speaking to Luc.'

Ah. 'So you know about his offer?'

'Yes.'

'And?'

'You know my feelings on getting involved with the Duvaliers, Gabrielle. On any level— no matter how small.'

'I thought I did,' she countered tartly. 'That was before Luc informed me that you and he had stayed in contact. What was that all about?'

'You,' said Rafael curtly. 'The first time he

called you were still on the plane to Australia. He wanted to check that I was meeting you. One thing Luc doesn't lack is a sense of responsibility. He wanted me to call him once you'd arrived safely. He wanted to know how you were every now and then. I saw no harm in telling him.'

'You told him I was a weeping, self-pitying wreck?' Gabrielle closed her eyes in mortification. 'Gee, thanks.'

'I told him you were fine,' said Rafe dryly. 'You know I'd never betray you.'

Gabrielle closed her eyes and rubbed at her forehead. Not game to speak for fear of the words on her tongue.

'How's Josien?' asked Rafe. 'Did she want to see you?'

'She'll live.' This she could talk about, never mind that there was no keeping the bitterness from her voice. 'And, no, she did not.'

Rafe didn't say I told you so. He didn't need to. 'You okay with that?' he asked gently.

'Which bit?' she said savagely, and let loose a black humoured chuckle of her own when Rafe laughed. 'Truly, Rafe, I'm fine.'

'Fine as in you're a weeping, self-pitying wreck, or fine as in fine?'

'Fine as in I've finally learned my lesson

and I'm moving on,' Gabrielle told him vehemently. 'Josien can't hurt me any more. I won't let her.'

'I like it,' said Rafe. 'There's something in your voice that makes me believe it.' His voice wrapped around her, familiar and comforting. 'Sometimes you've just got to let people go, Gabrielle. For your own sake.'

'I know.' Gabrielle took a deep and shuddering breath. *Don't go there*, a little voice whispered. *Don't even visit that place where fathers aren't fathers and Rafe is only half yours. Don't dwell there.* 'I've been looking at distribution options hereabouts,' she said in a stronger voice. 'Looking hard. It's not easy, Rafe. It's a closed system and I don't have the family name, the contacts or the leverage to open any doors. Luc's offer to let us hold a wine tasting for distributors at Caverness is a generous one and will open those doors. It could make a big difference to our entry point into the market. If there was no personal element to consider I'd be jumping all over his offer. It's exactly the kind of upmarket opportunity we need to start this ball rolling.'

Rafe said nothing.

'I haven't said yes,' said Gabrielle. 'I knew

Luc's offer wouldn't sit particularly well with you. I don't know that I'd feel all that comfortable doing business with him either. But I'd like you to consider it. As I'm doing.'

'I don't want his help.' Her brother's voice hardened. 'I do not want our business becoming entwined with that of the House of Duvalier.'

'Not even if it benefits us more than it benefits them?'

'Especially if it appears to benefit us more than it benefits them. They're not the most successful family-run champagne dynasty in France because of sheer dumb luck, Gabrielle. Luc's offering us this deal because he's after something.'

'Atonement?' suggested Gabrielle.

'You,' said Rafael bluntly. 'You're a grown woman, Gabrielle, and I know you can handle yourself. I just don't know if you can handle Luc. There's wildness in him underneath all that iron control. Always has been, always will be, and you've always called to it. He's always shielded you from it. Over and over I've watched him, Gabrielle. He was always so careful and controlled around you, always protecting you.'

'Protecting me from what?'

'Himself,' said Rafe.

'So he has a wild streak that he never indulges. So what? He'll be careful, I'll be careful, and we'll both be fine,' she said lightly. 'Have a little faith and don't let concern for me colour your decision. If the answer's still no once you've thought about it some more, so be it. I just want you to give it due consideration.'

'I can't,' he said gruffly. 'I know it makes good business sense, Gabrielle. But I can't do it.'

Gabrielle bit her lip and nodded, never mind that he couldn't see her. 'All right. That's all I needed to know.' Time to move on. 'I'm emailing you the details of an old vineyard that's for sale a few miles from Caverness. The old Hammerschmidt place—do you remember it?'

'The abandoned one?'

'You do remember it,' she said. 'I think it has potential.'

'To buy or to lease?'

'To buy.'

'So you still want to go back there to live? Even with Josien the way she is?'

'Yes,' said Gabrielle firmly. 'Josien has nothing to do with my decision to return. I

love it here, Rafe. I know you and Angels
Landing will always be there for me, but Australia doesn't call to me the way it calls to you.
It never has and it never will. I don't want you
to think I'm abandoning you—I would never
abandon you. I want you in my life. I need you
in it. You know that, don't you?'

'Here comes the but,' said Rafe gruffly.

'No buts,' she said, deliberately striving
for lightness. 'I want our wines to sell well
over here. I want to stay and work hard and
make that happen, but most of all, behind it
all…' she closed her eyes and let her heart
speak for her '…I just want to come home.'

CHAPTER SIX

'YOU'VE been avoiding me,' said Luc as he eased himself into the vacant wicker chair opposite Gabrielle.

Gabrielle looked up at him and tried to persuade her heart that he was just another charming rake of a man, no different from any other man and certainly no finer. She was sitting in a pavement café, a strong and sweet black coffee at her elbow and a folder containing potential properties for purchase spread out in front of her. A week had passed since she'd dined at Caverness. A long, frustrating week filled with a lot of hard work and no significant visible or calculable gain. Whatsoever.

'Why?' he said next, lounging back in his chair, a brooding, elegant presence as he surveyed her through bold black eyes.

'Maybe I've been working,' she said as she

closed the folder and sat back in her chair, glad of the dark sunglasses that covered her eyes and to some extent hid the heat in her cheeks. 'Maybe I haven't given you a second thought.'

'Maybe you haven't,' he said with a charming grin. 'And that would be depressing, considering how often I think of you.' He toyed with the menu, tossed it aside. 'I've arranged to tour the Hammerschmidt vineyard. I want to take a closer look at the soils and the vines. Would you care to join me?'

'To what end?' she said warily. Gabrielle did want to look over the old vineyard before it went to auction. She didn't necessarily think it was a good idea to do so with Luc. 'You're not really suggesting we do as Simone suggests and form a partnership, are you? Because I can't see it working for us.'

'Neither can I. Never mix business with pleasure, angel. And I do plan to pursue the pleasure angle.'

'So why look at this place together, then?'

'Because it would give us both an advantage over other bidders come auction day. They're asking twenty-two million euros for the property, Gabrielle. I can only see about thirteen million in assets that are of use to me. I want your opinion on its worth to someone with different plans for it.'

'So…this would be like a business meeting for us, as opposed to something more social?'

'Definitely,' said Luc. 'Although I'm not opposed to pleasure coming afterwards. I'm not opposed to sorting the pleasure element of the day out *now* so that we know where we stand on that particular subject. Have dinner with me.'

'Why?'

'Because you want to?' he offered.

'No, what I want to do is get a distribution network for our wines in place.'

Luc's eyes sharpened. 'All you have to do is ask.'

'If only it were that simple,' she murmured. 'I've spoken to Rafe about your offer to hold a wine tasting for us at Caverness.'

'I've spoken to him about that too,' said Luc. 'He didn't refuse. I took that as a good sign.'

'He didn't say yes,' Gabrielle felt obliged to point out. 'I think I can safely say that he's not likely to say yes any time in the near future. Just my sisterly opinion.' Backed by a definitive no. 'He's a little concerned about what might be in it for you.'

'I'm wounded by his cynicism,' said Luc. 'I'm also the tiniest bit impressed by it. My father always used to consider cynicism the mark of a clever businessman. What exactly does Rafe think I'm after?'

'Me,' she said dryly.

'Ah.'

'Is he wrong?'

Luc shrugged and his midnight eyes gleamed. 'I can't deny it—the thought of having you has crossed my mind. It's a very pleasurable thought. But my motives for helping you get your wines in front of the right people are a little more straightforward than that.' Luc's eyes lost that lazy gleam and shadows moved into place. 'My hands were tied all those years ago when Rafe asked for support. I wanted to go into partnership with him, offer him the House of Duvalier's backing. Phillipe did not. My father forced an ultimatum upon me. Rafe or Caverness. I chose Caverness.'

'Bastard,' muttered Gabrielle.

Luc smiled grimly. 'Me or my father?'

'Your father.'

'To him, it was just good business. Why

risk a reputation that had been generations in the making on an unknown? Why provide his only son with the distraction of another business to build when he needed me here?'

'So you're defending your father?'

'To some extent, yes. Rafe and I put him in an awkward position, Gabrielle. Seen through older, wiser eyes Phillipe did not deliberately set out to crush Rafael's dreams. We put a proposal to him which he refused. He made a business decision. A safe one. I do not steer as safe a course as my father, Gabrielle, but make no mistake, my offer is not based on sentiment alone. Yes, part of me simply wants to do for Rafael what I could not do before. The other part of me believes that offering patronage to the Angels Landing wines is simply good business. The wines are brilliant. The House of Duvalier's reputation will be enhanced because of the association and it's a market we don't currently cater to. If buyers wanted to source Angels Landing wines through the House of Duvalier, I would take my cut as a distributor.'

She believed him.

'And then there's you,' he said with a sigh that sounded more frustrated than lovelorn.

'I like to think of my attraction to you as a different problem altogether. I'm attracted to you and don't see why I should deny it. Our kiss in the garden suggests you're not exactly indifferent to me. The solution seems fairly straightforward.'

'You want me to become the *comte's* convenient mistress?'

'I'm not a *comte*,' he said. 'All I have is the castle.'

'All right, the billionaire's preferred plaything, then.'

'I'm not a billionaire either. Yet.' His lazy smile warned her it was on his to-do list. 'No, I want you to become my outrageously beautiful, independently wealthy lover.'

'Isn't that the same option?'

'No, you might have noticed that the wording's a little different.'

'They're just words, Luc. The outcome's the same.'

'It's an attitude thing.' He looked at her, his smile crookedly charming. 'So what do you say?'

To an affair with the likes of Luc Duvalier? 'I say it's dangerous. For both of us.'

Luc's eyes gleamed. 'There is that.'

'Not to mention insane,' she pointed out.

'Quite possibly. Was that a yes?'

She really didn't know what to say. She'd wanted to come back to the village a sophisticated, self assured, successful woman, and Luc was treating her exactly like one. No need to mention what a fake she felt. 'So how do we start this thing? If I were to agree to it. Which I haven't.' Yet.

'We start with dinner. Tonight. No expectations beyond a pleasant evening with fine food, fine wine and good company. And we see what happens.'

'I don't know,' she said, reaching for her coffee. 'It seems a little…'

'Straightforward?' he suggested. 'Civilised?'

'For us, yes,' she murmured. 'Where would we eat? Somewhere public or in private?'

'Somewhere public,' he said firmly. 'The restaurant I'm thinking of is a fine one—excellent food, small premises, and always busy. A man might take his lover there if he was trying to keep his hands off her.'

'Shall I meet you there?' she said.

'I will, of course, collect you,' he said, playing the autocrat and playing it well. *'Shall I meet you there,'* he murmured in disbelief. 'What kind of question is that?'

'Says the new-generation Frenchman,' she countered. 'Liberated, egalitarian, non-sexist…'

'Helpful, attentive, chivalrous…' he added with a reckless smile. 'And very beddable.'

He was that.

'All right,' she said. 'I'll give you the day—and tonight—to prove that a civilised and pleasurable and manageable affair wouldn't be beyond us. If you can prove this to my satisfaction, I'll make love with you. If this gets out of hand, however…'

'Yes?' he said silkily. 'What do you suggest?'

She leaned forward, elbows on the table. Luc leaned forward too. 'Well, I don't know about you,' she murmured, 'but I'm a clever, outrageously beautiful, independently wealthy woman. I plan to run.'

The real estate agent was not waiting for them when they pulled up at the gate to the Hammerschmidt Vineyard an hour later. Gabrielle glanced at Luc suspiciously, her suspicions turning to resignation as he cut the engine of the rumbling Audi and produced a massive set of keys from the centre console of the car. 'He was tied up with another sale when I saw him this morning,' said Luc. 'He said he might be running a little late.'

'So we wait for him?' said Gabrielle.

'No,' said Luc. Clearly, the master of Caverness waited for no man. 'We start without him.'

The Hammerschmidt vineyard comprised two hundred acres of prime grape-growing countryside of which less than half had been developed, underground storage caves, a few hundred wooden winemaking barrels in dreadful repair, old fashioned winemaking equipment, and a large two-storey house built in the Napoleonic style. The Hammerschmidts had played at winemaking for years, according to Luc, bankrolled by a seemingly endless supply of family money gained from the business of banking, which, rumour had it, they were extremely good at. They were not, according to Luc, particularly good at making champagne.

'So there's no reputation to be bought,' she said wryly.

'None whatsoever,' said Luc. 'The Hammerschmidt name is most definitely a liability. If you bought it, you'd rename it.'

'So what would you call it?'

'I think Folly' he said. 'Because whoever buys it is definitely going to be half mad.'

'Angels Curse?' she said. 'No, too dark. Angels Falling?' Gabrielle frowned. 'Possibly a little bit downbeat. Angels Wings? Angels Flying? There. That one could work. Nice tie-in to the core business. Kind of uplifting.' She stared out over the old vineyard. 'Because, boy, does this need lifting up.'

'If ever you're looking for marketing work, call me,' said Luc. 'I would love to let you and Simone loose on a House of Duvalier campaign.'

'So much blind faith,' said Gabrielle airily, but her head ballooned from the compliment, putting a spring in her step and a smile on her lips. 'So how long has this place been on the market?'

'Six months,' said Luc. 'But it's been vacant ten years or more. The vermin have taken up residence, along with the pests. It's a mess.'

According to Luc, the people hereabouts were more than ready to see someone who knew what they were doing take over the vineyard.

That someone being him.

If she were a neighbour she'd be all for the House of Duvalier coming in here with their money, knowledge, reputation, and the wherewithal to set this place to rights too.

The house took Gabrielle completely by surprise. Simone had called it a wreck. It wasn't.

'It's beautiful,' she said in wonder.

'It's a façade,' said Luc. 'Wait until you step inside. The house is uninhabitable.' Luc punctuated his words with the turn of the door key in the lock before putting the shoulder of his immaculate suit to the door and shoving hard. The door gave way but not by much. There seemed to be a build-up of garden debris behind it, garden debris that rustled even as Gabrielle stepped back and leaned down to peer into the pile from a safe distance away. Australia had taught her the value of being wary of those things that rustled in the undergrowth. Things that rustled in the undergrowth in Australia had a habit of being dangerous, if not lethal.

A narrow black nose appeared, followed by the sweetest little face imaginable, dominated by liquid brown eyes and surrounded by needle-sharp spines. With sleepy dignity the hedgehog made its way to the front door and peered outside before turning and ambling back down the darkened corridor. The garden debris rustled again and a miniature version of the first hedgehog followed.

'Well, maybe not *completely* uninhabitable,' said Gabrielle and grinned when Luc gave her one of those looks that suggested she was being ridiculous.

'After you,' he said, the epitome of good manners.

Gabrielle looked at her shoes, then looked at the hedgehog nest. 'Are you sure you wouldn't like to carry me over the threshold? Because, by all means, feel free.'

'That would involve touching you,' said Luc, 'and we both know that's never a good idea.'

'I'm curious,' said Gabrielle as she carefully picked her way through the hedgehog house. 'How do you plan to conduct this civilised affair without ever actually touching me?'

'I didn't say I *wouldn't* be touching you,' he said. 'I have touching plans. But the time between that first touch and being, for want of a better description, all over you, won't be very long. I'm pacing myself. Waiting for the right moment.' Gabrielle stepped on something slippery and wobbled alarmingly before putting her hand to the wall to steady herself. Luc put one of his hands to her waist.

She stepped away quickly. Luc let go fast, as if he'd been burnt.

'That wasn't it,' he murmured. 'A civilised man would not make love to a woman in a ruined *manoir*.'

'How very thoughtful of you.'

'I know,' he said. 'The things I have planned very definitely require a bed.'

Gabrielle closed her eyes and suppressed a needy whimper. If he kept talking in that low liquid voice about the things he might require from a lover, she for one wouldn't be needing a bed. 'What kind of things?' she whispered helplessly.

'Wicked things.' His voice rumbled through her. 'Wanton things.' She bit her lip as her breasts responded to the caress in his words, tightening, peaking, aching for his touch.

'Stop,' she begged. 'Lucien, please. Not here.' When she opened her eyes he was staring down at her, his grin rueful and his eyes dark with need.

'Stopping is something we won't be doing, I guarantee it. I'm seriously considering laying in a week's worth of supplies beforehand.'

Only a week's worth? Gabrielle had seven years' worth of longing for this man to ride out. It was going to take longer than a week.

'We, ah, should probably try and keep interruptions to a minimum,' she said.

Luc's smile had more than a hint of the devil in it. 'I like your forethought.'

'Clear the decks of any pressing items of business,' she continued.

'You are so right,' he murmured. 'Shall we get on with the tour?'

Oh, yeah. This tour.

It didn't take more than half a dozen steps down the hallway for Gabrielle to concede that Luc hadn't been exaggerating when he'd said that the inside of the house was a disaster. There was mould on the ceilings, dampness seeping up through the walls, leaks in the roof, and window drapes that should have been burned a hundred years ago if only to prevent the onset of plague. Ivy clawed at once glorious French windows, seeking purchase and finding it in the window cracks and joints. The ground floor flooring was a dull and pitted marble, the upper storey floorboards felt spongy in places where the rot had taken hold. The stairs were unsafe, the elaborate wrought-iron balustrade rickety, and as for the kitchen… The state of the kitchen was enough to make anyone who took pride in the preparing of food weep with despair.

'Maybe after a good clean…' she said, and winced at Luc's steady glance that told her he wasn't even going to dignify her comment with a reply. 'Okay, so it needs work,' she muttered.

'No, it needs bulldozing.'

'But the façade…' That beautiful Napoleonic façade.

'All right, hold the bulldozer, but it still needs gutting. The façade you're so enamoured of needs extensive and expensive restoration and the inside of the house needs rebuilding. Am I wrong? Because—' he spread his arms wide to encompass the large upstairs room they were currently standing in '—I don't think I'm wrong.'

'You're right,' she said. 'You're absolutely right. It's just…' The rooms were so splendidly proportioned, with their high ceilings and their tall French windows. With the heavy drapes gone the natural lighting within the house would be superb. The view from this window alone made Gabrielle sigh with pleasure and Luc sigh with something else entirely.

'It needs a lot of work, Gabrielle, and deep, deep pockets,' he warned.

'I know,' she said with another wistful sigh. 'There's really not a lot to recommend it, is there? Except for the hedgehogs—the hedgehogs were cute.' The distinct odour of mice and other vermin hinted that the hedgehogs weren't the only inhabitants of Hammerschmidt Manoir. 'On the bright side, the state of the house should bring the value of the property down considerably. I think even a builder would think twice about taking on a project house like this one. Whoever buys this place will be after the land—like you. The house is a liability.'

'Does that mean you're not interested in the property?'

Gabrielle shot him a lightning grin. 'I didn't say that. I still want to see the wine-making equipment and the storage caves.'

Like the house, the winemaking and storage areas were without power. Luckily for them, Luc had a torch.

'Boy scout,' she said.

'Not ever, and well you know it,' he countered. He'd run wild as a boy, they all had; the chateau and the land surrounding it had encouraged children that way. But he had grown up with the caves of Caverness at his back, hence the torch. He probably had spare batteries and quite possibly another torch tucked away somewhere on his most spectacular person. Not that Gabrielle felt inclined to examine him and find out.

Luc's 'no casual touching' rule suited her fine. Just, her fingers twitched, fine.

'How far into the caves do you want to go?' he asked, flicking torchlight around the entrance tunnel once he'd shifted the rusting wrought-iron gate aside.

'Not far.' The well-lit and equally well-mapped caves of Caverness were one thing, a maze of abandoned underground tunnels was quite another. 'After you.'

'Ladies first,' he murmured.

'You are such a gentleman.' Swiping the torch from Luc's unresisting fingers Gabrielle lifted her chin high and started into the darkness, with Luc a few steps behind her, chuckling softly.

'So…' he said as she shone the torchlight high. 'Still scared of bats?'

'No,' she said loftily. 'I've outgrown that particular fear.' Mind you, it never hurt to send a prayer of silent thanks that there were no bats hanging from the roof of this particular grotto. At least, none in torch range. She swung the thready beam of light downwards fast; it was probably best not to know.

Gabrielle shivered as they moved further into the tunnel and the temperature plummeted. Luc was wearing a suit. Gabrielle wore a thin cotton blouse.

'Cold?' murmured Luc silkily.

'Not at all.'

'So if you're not scared and you're not cold, why is the torch trembling?'

Ah. That. 'Probably a fault in the wiring.' Something rustled beneath her feet and Gabrielle lost all pretence of bravery as she shot one hand out to grasp hold of Luc by his shirtfront and pointed the torch towards her feet with the other. 'What was that?'

'Me choking on my shirt collar?' he suggested dryly.

Oh. She released her grip and smoothed his shirt back in place for good measure, but she did not step away. 'Stay close.'

'I am close.'

He also had another torch in his pocket, which he withdrew and switched on, adding its glow to the light coming from her own, sweeping it back and forth along the floor of the cave.

'Whatever it was, it's gone,' he said, and with a wider sweep of his torch, 'This isn't a bad storage area, Gabrielle. Look, it's high, dry, good sized, and it smells well ventilated. Add a solid door rather than the wrought-iron gate at the entrance and install some lighting and you'd have good temperature control in here year round.'

'Are there any more caverns like this?'

Luc the intrepid stepped forward, Gabrielle followed, making sure she stayed within arm's length and only bumping into him twice. She kept one hand on his back after that, and to hell with not touching him until they were ready to make love for a week. That particular rule only applied outside underground caves potentially crawling with rats and harbouring bats.

The Hammerschmidt grottos boasted three more vast caverns, each one larger than the last. Storage enough for ten years' worth of Angels Landing harvests, decided Gabrielle, with the potential to excavate deeper underground as needed. With very little effort the caves could be made useable and very easily rentable.

'Seen enough?' murmured Luc.

She had. The caves were an asset—no

question. They could talk their merits to death later, but for now the cold had seeped into her bones, she was shivering uncontrollably, and warmth and sunshine were high on her list of priorities.

'Hold this,' said Luc and thrust his torch into the hand at his back. The next minute a jacket fell around her shoulders, warm from the wearing and bearing the unmistakable scent of Luc. He took back the torch and took her hand and headed back the way they'd come in.

Once outside he stood her in the sun and stared down at her broodingly. 'You never did have any sense when it came to the caves,' he said gruffly. 'Warmer now?'

'M-much,' she managed.

'You want me to warm you?'

'N-not unless you're free all n-next week, n-no.'

'So can I have my jacket back?'

'Over m-my dead body.' Which could be a possibility if he attempted to take his jacket from her. She glared at him and tucked her arms in the sleeves for good measure, this time suppressing a shiver of pure delight as Luc's warmth wrapped around her. 'Exercise,' she said. 'Exercise will warm me up. Let's take a look at the vines.'

'You want to walk them or run them?' he said with the tilt of his lips. They'd run the fields as children, she, Luc, and Rafael. Rafe had always given her twenty rows' head start. Luc had been known to give her thirty and still catch her at the finish line.

'I'd rather walk,' she said and suited actions to words. Luc fell into step beside her, keeping a careful distance between them, a distance he hadn't enforced in the caves.

'Are you trying to keep your hands off me, Luc?'

'Not trying,' he murmured. 'I *am* keeping my hands off you.' He glanced skywards as if for heavenly support. 'I can't believe you haven't noticed.'

Gabrielle grinned and then stopped abruptly as they came upon the first row of vines. The grapes, unpruned, uncared for, and full of disease, were a disaster. The thorny, rambling monsters planted at the end of each row of vines looked vaguely familiar but they didn't look like grapes. 'Are these...roses?'

'Got it in one,' said Luc dryly.

She looked along the rows of wire that supposedly supported the vines and currently supported Rosacea's finest. 'But who in their right mind would plant rambling roses amongst the vines?'

'No one,' he said darkly.

'Pretty though.'

He looked at her as if she'd grown another head. Gabrielle sniggered. 'What would you do with these vines?'

'Rip them out and replant.'

'And the trellis?' The wood and wire framework had to be at least a hundred years old.

'That would go too.'

'Expensive,' she murmured.

'Very.'

'You'd be better off starting from scratch.'

'Don't tempt me,' he said. 'The land is perfectly sloped for the sun on the grapes and it's close to Caverness. They're big pluses.'

'Yes, but do they match the big drawbacks?'

'I haven't decided yet.'

Neither had Gabrielle. 'It could have been so good,' she said.

'Let the hedgehog be a warning to you,' he countered, with a crooked grin that warmed her the way his coat had. 'Let's talk about it some more over lunch.'

'Lunch where?'

'I know a place you'll like,' he said. 'It's in the hills.' And when she hesitated. 'It's only lunch, Gabrielle. Save your hesitation for dinner.'

Well, when he put it like that…

'Very nice,' said Gabrielle as they were seated at an outdoor table of an elegant hotel café nestled into the hills of Champagne. Minutes later a pitcher of iced water had joined the party, accompanied by a chilled glass of white wine for Gabrielle and a foaming brown beer for Luc. The café was famed for its selection of sour dark breads and cheeses as well as for the views of the countryside from its hillside terrace. A cheese and pâté platter would be joining them directly. Luc had ordered it. Gabrielle's mouth watered at the thought of it but she turned her attention to her surroundings until it turned up.

'The view from the hill behind Caverness is better,' she commented idly. 'Ever thought of putting a café up there?'

'No.'

'Because it wouldn't be economically viable?'

'No, because I like the hilltop as it is.'

'So you're not always all about business?'

Crinkles framed Luc's eyes. A smile lurked nearby. 'Never have been.'

'And yet the House of Duvalier thrives under your rule.'

'I never said I wasn't good at what I do, Gabrielle. I am.'

'If you hadn't inherited the family dynasty what would you have done?' she asked curiously.

'You mean after the fighter pilot phase and the *medicines-sans-frontiers* phase had ended?'

'Yes,' she said with the tilt of her lips. 'After you'd finished with those particular adventures.' Luc's dreams always had been adventurous, even when they'd been children. Not for him boring games like cowboys and Indians. No, when they'd played make believe they'd been World War Two resistance fighters smuggling refugees to safety or World War One aces trying to outmanoeuvre the Red Baron, with Rafael the Baron and Simone and Gabrielle Luc's wingmen. 'We never did catch that Red Baron, did we?'

If Luc had trouble keeping up with the conversation he didn't let it show. 'Simone caught him once.'

'Only because Rafe let her.'

'No, she bested him. I saw it all. Rafe only

pretended that he'd let her catch him. Even a twelve year old has his pride. But she out-thought him, fair and square.' Luc sounded more than a little proud of his sister and so he should be. As a youth Rafe had had more evasive manoeuvres up his sleeve than many a world leader. He still did.

'If you ask me, Rafe fell a little bit in love with her that day,' said Luc with a wry smile. 'And whenever Simone surprised him after that, or shielded you from Josien's wrath, he fell in love with her that little bit more. He's loyal, Rafe. To you. Even to Josien, in his way. He'd have worked his heart out for Simone had she gone to Australia with him.'

'Then how come you didn't say that seven years ago?' muttered Gabrielle. She didn't mean to sound accusing. She didn't want to argue with Luc about Simone and Rafe's disastrous relationship, but her words were sharper than she'd intended.

'You think I didn't?'

'I think you made like Switzerland and tried to be neutral.'

'What if I did?' he said mildly, but his eyes were guarded. 'Simone was eighteen and born to a life of luxury. Rafe was twenty-two, penniless, and about to move halfway across the world on a whim. He had nothing to offer her but love and a determination to succeed that bordered on obsessive. I care for Rafe like a brother but that doesn't mean I'm blind to his faults. I'm not blind to Simone's either. Would you have had me say that I thought Simone too demanding and immature to lead the life Rafe wanted her to lead? Would you have had me accuse Rafe of being too driven to succeed to be able to afford a wife at that time? You supported Rafe, Gabrielle, and I was glad of it. But you only saw the romance, not the enormity of what Rafe asked of my sister.'

'He asked her to *believe* in him,' she said heatedly. 'Is that so wrong?'

'He asked her to forgo her family and her inheritance for him, Gabrielle. There was no middle ground with Rafe. No compromise. He was leaving and Simone could either go with him or it was over.'

'You don't know what it was like for Rafe here,' said Gabrielle raggedly. 'Josien's hatred for him was like a cancer, eating away at every plan and hope he ever entertained. If Rafe hadn't left here when he did, Josien would have destroyed him. He *couldn't* stay.'

Luc's eyes had darkened, whether with

temper or with sorrow she couldn't fathom. 'I know,' he said simply. 'And Simone could not leave. Can't you see that?'

She could. She did. And she hated seeing it laid out so clearly, every fault line and crevasse exposed. 'I don't even know how we came to be arguing about this,' she muttered. 'It's just…I see Simone so careful with her questions about my life in Australia, with her feelings still so raw, even after all these years. I see Rafe who can't even bring himself to speak her name, and all I want to do is make their pain go away.'

'You can't,' said Luc gently. 'Only they can do that, and only when they're ready. It's the way of love, and of life.'

'When did you get so wise?' she asked, shooting him a half-hearted glare.

'I've always been wise,' he countered. 'You just never noticed.'

A tiny smile escaped her. 'I was probably too busy noticing other things about you. Sixteen-year-old girls don't necessarily look for wisdom in a beau.'

'No?' He looked intrigued. 'What did you look for?'

'Beauty,' she said. 'Which you had in spades. Mystery, which you had as well, never mind that I'd known you all my life. Danger, which I could always sense in you but never saw in action. Sexuality. I trust I'm not the only woman to ever tell you that you have that one covered. And weakness. I looked for that too.'

'And did you find any?'

'You were chivalrous. Protective to a fault and I played on that. Used it to make you notice me. I called it weakness back then and I planned my seduction of you around it.'

'Brat,' he said without heat.

'I know,' she admitted readily enough. 'And foolish with it. I would not necessarily call a man's protective streak a weakness *now*.'

'No?' The cheese platter came and Luc thanked the waiter in acknowledgement. 'What would you call it?'

To a woman who could have done with a whole lot more love and protection as a child? She perused the cheeses. 'Practically irresistible.'

His smile came slow and sweet, with only a hint of the sexual wattage she knew Luc was capable of. Such charming restraint. Such exemplary behaviour. He'd promised her as much, she'd demanded nothing less of him. The problem was that deep down inside she didn't want Luc the civil and well-behaved suitor. No, she wanted the other Luc. The one who could not, and would not, be tamed. She knew he was in there. And, as dangerous as that Luc was to her well-being, that small reckless voice inside her wanted him to come out and play.

'You're looking very thoughtful,' he murmured.

'Am I?' She was feeling very wanton. 'I'm just rethinking my plans for the afternoon. I've a couple of tasks to see to before dinner.'

'I'll return you to the village after we've finished up here,' he told her. 'Will that give you enough time to see to them?'

'I think so.' She'd never preplanned wanton behaviour before but surely it wouldn't take more than a couple of hours.

Luc turned the wattage up on that lazy smile. 'Have I been manageable enough for you this morning?'

'Yes, indeed. Your meekness and self restraint have been a wonder to behold.'

'I know.' His smile was anything but meek and Gabrielle gloried in it. 'Are we still on for dinner?'

'Yes.' Madness notwithstanding, she'd made her decision. She would join Luc for dinner and dress to please a man and see if she could put a dint in all that iron self-control. 'Yes, we are.'

'I've formulated a plan,' Gabrielle told Simone later that afternoon over a glass of wine at Simone's favourite café.

'What kind of plan?' asked Simone, looking sun-spelled and feline-lazy.

'A plan for exploring my physical attraction to Luc. I'm figuring to encourage that particular aspect of our relationship along somewhat. Get it over and done with, so to speak, so that I can stop *thinking* about it so much and get back to concentrating on my work.'

Simone turned her head and looked at Gabrielle from over the rim of her sunglasses. 'Hnh,' she said finally.

'The thing is, I'm a little nervous about heading out to dinner with a man whose mind I intend to mess with.'

'So you should be,' said Simone.

'Looking for a little support here,' murmured Gabrielle. 'Possibly a little help. I need to know what a woman should do when she wants to drive a man insane with lust.'

'She should *not* ask the man's sister how to go about it,' said Simone dryly. 'There are some things a sister simply can't, or won't, help you with.'

'You're right. My apologies. That was thoughtless of me.' Gabrielle drummed her fingers on the café table top. 'Suppose I were to ask you for more generic advice about heading out to dinner with a man I wanted to seduce. Advice not targeted towards any one individual in particular. Would you have any suggestions on how to go about it then?'

'But of course,' said Simone. 'That's a different request altogether.'

'Excellent. So where does one begin?'

'You'll need a dress.'

'I have a dress.'

'I never doubted it for a moment,' said Simone. 'You'll also need a coat to go over this dress. The reveal is very important.'

True, so very true. 'When would you say was the best time for this reveal to happen?'

'Somewhere public. Somewhere where many eyes will be drawn to you. I'm very fond of making a man feel possessive. Of course, I should warn you that if we were talking about Lucien I would encourage you to skip that step altogether. He's always been possessive of you and needs no further encouragement in that direction.'

'What about a bunch of little reveals throughout the evening, just to keep his attention? A wrist here, a hint of perfume there.'

'Perfect.'

'Then what?'

'Banter.'

'Sexual?'

'Sophisticated.' Simone shook her head. 'I swear, Australia has had an unforgivable influence on you. Where's your sense of subtlety?'

'Okay, sophisticated and subtly sexual banter.'

'No, no, no!' said Simone. 'A woman intent on driving a man mad with lust does not talk of sex at all! All she need do is imagine the sex.'

'I'm not sure that particular piece of advice is going to work for me.' Imagining sex with Luc tended to fry her brain. Attempting sophisticated non-sexual banter while frying her brain could prove quite a stretch.

'No one said this was going to be *easy*,' said Simone dryly. 'Seduction is an art, and like any form of art it requires commitment, constant practice, and skill.'

'Okay, I'll use my imagination. Then what?'

'Pheromones,' said Simone sagely. 'Do not underestimate them.'

'Pheromones. Right. Good to know. I'm not even going to ask you how you know this stuff. Anything else?'

'Yes. Seduction isn't a game so never, ever treat it as one. Seduction is war.'

'War,' echoed Gabrielle. 'Not an art form?'

'So much to learn,' said Simone on a pitying sigh. 'So little time.'

'I'm a little uncomfortable with seduction as war,' argued Gabrielle. 'Couldn't seduction be a duel instead?'

'All right, seduction is a duel,' said Simone with an airy wave of her hand. 'You'll be wanting the points on the blades removed next.'

'I *do* want them removed,' she said earnestly. 'I don't want to hurt anyone, Simone. Especially not the person I intend to seduce. That's not part of the plan.'

'I'm relieved to hear it, all things considered, but the fact remains that I've just armed you with a blade. The traditional use of any blade is to force the acquisition of something that would not otherwise be freely given. The traditional response to such a weapon is surrender, but not always. Sometimes the wielder of the blade gets more than they bargained for.'

Gabrielle contemplated Simone's words. 'I'll be careful,' she said finally.

'I hope so.' Simone studied her pensively. 'I started out in this conversation feeling protective of Luc. Now I'm sitting here wondering how on earth I'm going to protect *you*. You're out of your depth, Gabrielle. Luc knows how to fascinate women. I believe he knows obsession. He's felt the sting of it before. For you. I doubt he'll play at seduction with a blunted blade the way you intend to. Are you *really* ready for this?'

Gabrielle gave the question the attention it deserved. 'I'll be *very* careful,' she said finally.

Simone sighed heavily. 'I hope you know what you're doing, Gabrielle, because I don't want to lose you again.' She looked broodingly at her near-empty wine glass. 'Either of you.'

Lucien dressed carefully for his dinner date that evening. Not a suit, no, a suit was too formal, but a pair of suede trousers and a favoured casual shirt, soft to the touch and tailored to his physique. His watch had an antique gold face and a brown leather band and was also one of his favourites. A person had to know watches to know that it was Cartier. The cufflinks with the Duvalier crest he was undecided about. On the one hand, this was who he was. On the other hand, Gabrielle's relationship with Caverness and the House of Duvalier was somewhat stormy.

He needed advice. Female advice.

'What do you think?' he asked when he cornered Simone in the television room. He held up the cufflinks. 'Yes or no?'

'More information required,' said Simone. 'Where are you going?'

'Out for a meal. A casual, informal, getting to know you meal.'

'With a woman?'

'Yes.'

'A woman you wish to impress?'

'Not exactly *impress*,' he said. 'This woman knows me already. She's probably not all that impressable.'

'Don't wear them, then,' said Simone. 'Give the House of Duvalier the night off. That is, unless you'd rather wear them and feel secure in the knowledge that your shirt won't be coming off in a hurry.'

'My shirt isn't going to come off at all,' said Luc darkly, and set to threading the cufflinks through his cuffs. 'Tonight isn't about seduction. Tonight is all about showing restraint.'

'Pardon?' said Simone.

An incredulous pardon if ever he'd heard one. 'Restraint,' he said again.

'Hnh,' said Simone, but by the time he looked up from fastening his cuffs she'd turned back to her book. Luc sighed at her impressively short attention span and decidedly unsisterly concern for his needs.

'So, let's say I did want to make sure that the evening was a pleasant non-sexual one for all concerned. What do I do?'

Simone lowered her book with a sigh. 'What do you usually do?'

'Pleasantly non sexual isn't exactly in my repertoire,' he confided. 'Hence the need for advice.'

'Is Gabrielle the woman you're intending to have this pleasantly platonic evening with?'

'Possibly,' said Luc. 'Probably. Although there's no need for your advice to be specifically tailored to Gabrielle. Generic advice will do. You never know when a few pleasant platonics will come in handy.'

'You have no idea how underprepared I am for this conversation,' said Simone darkly.

'Well, if you don't know, just say so,' he began, but stopped when she held up her hand.

'I'm thinking…' she said. 'Just give me a moment.'

He gave her two. 'Well?'

'Well…since you asked so nicely and waited so patiently for me to collect my thoughts, I'll share a few ideas I have on the subject.'

'Appreciated,' he said.

Amusement slid through Simone's gleaming gaze. 'I recommend ignoring outright any moves laden with subtly sexual overtones.'

'Ignore them,' said Luc with a puzzled frown. 'As in…*ignore* them? Really?'

'Completely,' said Simone. 'Act as if they never happened. If a woman greets you in a dress designed to destroy a man, smile in an easy and open fashion, comment on the suitability of the weather, and ask her if she likes puppies.'

'Puppies?' echoed Luc.

'Puppies,' she said firmly. 'Not kittens. Stay away from the kitten talk—you never know where that one might lead. Keep the conversation grounded. Nothing too sophisticated. Something casual and feel-good without being threatening. Puppies are perfect.' She eyed him speculatively. 'It's a pity you didn't come to me earlier with this. I could have arranged for you to borrow one.'

Borrow a puppy? Four bounding legs, sweeping tail, floppy ears, liquid eyes, and a wet, inquisitive nose? His sister had gone insane. 'Thank you, but no.'

'You also need to do a little something with your hair.'

'My hair? What's wrong with my hair?'

'Well, it's falling all over your face and needs cutting for starters, but apart from that a woman's going to take one look at it and want to run her fingers through it. Tie it back. Like a soccer star or a scorpion king. Trust me, your features won't suffer for it.'

'*What?*' He really wasn't keeping up with the gist of this conversation at all.

'I'll lend you a black leather band. Very manly.'

'Won't pulling my hair back make a woman want to rearrange it?' Luc didn't know a lot about how a man's hair affected a woman's fingers but he knew enough about his own reaction to a woman's tresses to know that whenever they put it up, he rarely rested until he'd taken every last pin and hairband *out*.

'Not at all,' said Simone blithely. 'Where's your coat?'

'Do I need a coat?'

'But of course you need a coat. A coat makes you look solid and dependable. You should keep it on. You should probably make your companion keep hers on too. Just a nice platonic dinner between two people wearing coats and talking puppies. Not a lot to get excited about there.'

No, thought Luc with the first faint stirrings of unease. There wasn't. 'Anything else?'

'Isn't that enough?'

She was probably right. 'Well, thanks for the advice.'

'You know me.' Simone favoured him with a sisterly smile. 'Always happy to help.'

CHAPTER SEVEN

Luc's dinner date with Gabrielle started well. He wore a coat. She met him at the door to her apartment and, lo, she happened to be wearing a coat also. A severe black leather three-quarter-length, double-breasted coat cinched tightly at the waist with a wide black belt. Her black leather purse had a severe Prada look about it, and her hair had been scraped off her face into a no-nonsense schoolmarm bun with not a wayward tendril in sight. Luc's fingers began to itch, but he shoved them in his coat pocket and thought of puppies. He stepped back to let her by as she shut the door and brushed past him towards the narrow garden path. He glanced downwards to make sure she was minding her step on the uneven cobbles and all coherent thought fled. Gabrielle's shoes were black like the rest of her attire, but there the resemblance to the rest of her attire ended. The elegant four-inch stilettos owed nothing to practicality, severity, or plainness. These shoes had one purpose and one purpose only.

To bring a man to his knees.

'St Bernards,' he muttered.

'What?'

'Puppies. St Bernard puppies. I saw some today. I'm thinking of getting one.'

'You?' she said sceptically. 'And a puppy.'

'Yes.'

'At Caverness.'

'Yes.'

'Josien will be pleased,' said Gabrielle dryly.

'For company,' he said, suddenly inspired. 'He could sit at my feet on those long winter nights, in front of the fire while I…' While he what?

'Rest?' supplied Gabrielle.

'Yes, rest, and maybe do a spot of reading. The Napoleonic Wars, The Battle of Waterloo, that sort of thing.' Did that sound platonic and non-sexual enough? 'The Joy of Shoes.'

'The what?'

'The Joy of Choux. It's about pastry. You haven't read it?' Pastry… Puppies… Whatever. He figured they were interchangeable.

Gabrielle sent him a very steady stare. 'Have you been drinking?'

'Not yet.' Although those shoes could doubtless drive a man to it.

'And what happened to your hair?'

'What do you mean?' He narrowly resisted putting his hand to his recently curtailed locks.

'Where is it?'

As far as he *knew*, the hair that usually fell around his face was currently tied high on the back of his head, Soccer Striker or Scorpion King style. Not that he was either. 'Simone tells me it takes a man of pure courage to wear his hair like this.'

'I'm sure she did,' murmured Gabrielle. 'Did she tell you it takes a man of outstanding beauty to carry it off?'

She hadn't.

'Fortunately, you've got that one covered as well,' she said next with somewhat grudging appreciation. 'Tell her I approve. My fantasy life may never be the same.'

Was that sexual innuendo? It could have been. Luc decided to ignore it anyway, just to be on the safe side. They'd been doing so well. Right up until her shoes and his hair.

'Tell you what,' he offered. 'You take your hair down and I'll do the same with mine.'

'Have you any idea how long it took the hairdresser to put my hair *up*?' said Gabrielle eyeing him narrowly.

'Two minutes?' Not according to the look on her face. 'Five minutes?' His fingers really itched. 'Okay, ten. But I swear I could turn it loose for you in no time at all.'

'Luc…' She raised a stern yet delightfully elegant hand in his direction. 'Don't touch.'

'Good idea.' *Good* idea. He was in desperate need of more platonic conversation. 'You know, a puppy would have a field day with your shoes.'

Gabrielle looked down at her shoes and did that thing women did with their bodies when trying on clothes, or in this case shoes. The tiny turns and twists while they studied the item in question from every conceivable angle. 'What's wrong with my shoes?'

Oh, nothing a black lace corset and matching panties wouldn't fix. 'All those skinny little straps. All that space in between.' Crimson toenails. He'd never before paid particular attention to the colour of a woman's toenails but he seemed to be spending a great deal of time studying these ones. 'They seem a bit insubstantial, that's all.'

'Not for a restaurant, surely,' she countered sweetly as she straightened and smoothed her coat back into place with similarly crimson-tipped hands. 'It's not as if we're going to be mountain climbing.' Her smile was just this side of wicked. 'A man like you will be no doubt thinking of saving that particular joy for your mountain-loving puppy.'

She swept past him with another blinding smile and her chin held high, the rest of her swathed in punishment black. A waft of something floral and French teased at his nostrils, one of the newer, younger fragrances that snuck up on a man and wrapped around him when he least expected it. Or maybe that was just Gabrielle.

They made it to the car, to the restaurant, to the door of the restaurant without catastrophe. They stepped inside and warmth and the aroma of good food chased away the elusive scent of the woman at his side. The restaurant wasn't a large one, it seated thirty perhaps, but Luc knew from experience that every table would be filled before the night was through and that it wasn't unusual for the wait staff to book both early and late sittings for the same table space.

The room was small and narrow, a red leather bench seat ran the length of one wall, allowing closely placed tables for two or four to slot in next. Plain cushioned restaurant chairs had been placed on the other side of the tables. A narrow pathway down the middle of the room served as the food highway, and a scattering of slightly more private tables graced the other side of the room. The bar stood to the back of the room, the kitchen was situated behind that. A coat rack stood by the door. Gabrielle hesitated and her hands went to the belt at her waist.

'It's warm in here,' she murmured.

Yes, it was. Luc's hands went automatically to her shoulders to help with the removal of her coat before he remembered Simone's suggestion about keeping coats on. 'It'll be cooler by the window,' he said. 'You don't want to take a seat and see if you're more comfortable with your coat on?'

'No.' But she looked undecided. 'No one else is wearing their coats in here.'

True. The coat rack was currently groaning beneath the weight of discarded outerwear. One of Gabrielle's shoulders appeared, and then another. Two shoulders and an expanse of smooth and creamy skin. Luc swallowed hard. What *was* she almost wearing?

Something strapless, obviously. Strapless

and crimson—a deep blood-wine red—
Gabrielle's dress clung lovingly to every
perfect inch of her hourglass figure and
finished somewhere around mid-thigh.

'Rottweilers,' he whimpered.

'What about them?' Gabrielle turned and
slanted him a look through eyes that knew
only too well the effect such a dress was
likely to have on a man.

'Could be useful protection for the
chateau,' he said, dragging his gaze away
from the curve of her neck and the pins in her
hair before restless fingers got the better of
him. He parked her coat on the rack and
followed it up with his own.

'Mmm,' said Gabrielle. 'They could keep
your St Bernard company.'

Luc didn't even attempt an answer. He was
too busy staring down the myriad admiring
glances coming Gabrielle's way. 'I swear, if
I'd known what you were wearing before we
left your apartment we wouldn't have been
going anywhere,' he muttered darkly,
scowling at a local brewery owner who'd
shown the bad sense to stare at Gabrielle in
open appreciation. The man nodded to him
in recognition, his grin widening. Luc put
his hand to the small of Gabrielle's back.

Mine, said the gesture, and he didn't care who knew it. 'Shall we be seated or would you care for a drink at the bar first?'

Gabrielle looked at the barstools while Luc pondered the elasticity of that perfectly fitted dress. Clearly there would be no sitting on a barstool for Gabrielle. Not unless she wanted to be dragged from the restaurant and plastered against the wall of the nearest dark alleyway while he slaked his thirst and made sure those endless legs were wrapped around him. They might make it to the alleyway, he thought grimly. If they were lucky.

'A table, I think,' she said with a smile.

'*Good* call.' He was a man on the edge, and everyone in the restaurant but Gabrielle seemed to know it. The people he knew smiled and nodded and looked away fast, as if sensing the unpredictability of his next move.

The elderly, slightly built dark-haired waiter headed their way fast as well. There was a ripple in the fabric of the atmosphere of his room and he wanted it smoothed.

'Monsieur Duvalier, always a pleasure. A table by the window for yourself and the *mademoiselle*?' The waiter was eyeing Gabrielle with a careful smile and a forehead full of frownlines. 'Mademoiselle Gabrielle?'

'Paolo?'

'*Oui!*' Paolo beamed. 'You remembered.'

'Of course I remembered.' Gabrielle's smile was conspiratorial. 'Saturdays, Sundays, and Mondays. The bread run. You delivered the baguettes from a basket on your pushbike.'

'I tried.' Paolo glanced at Luc. 'Not that I ever made it to the kitchen door. Always her mother would send her tearing down the laneway to meet me. I missed you once you left, *chica*. There was no one left to save my poor legs the climb.'

Gabrielle smiled. 'Do you still have the bread run?'

'But no. The bread run bought this business. My son, he became a chef and does the cooking, and *his* sons work as kitchen hands. This old man is content to wait tables. With good word of mouth and excellent patronage, old Paolo's family prospers.'

'Bravo,' said Gabrielle softly as Paolo seated them at a table by the window and disappeared, returning shortly thereafter with a jug of iced water, a tiny bowl of olives dipped in herb oil and a basket of fresh and crusty bread.

'It is fortunate you chose this evening to dine with us,' Paolo told Luc as he draped first Gabrielle's napkin across her lap and then Luc's across his. 'A case of the 1976 Saracenne Reserve Brut arrived this morning and has spent the entire day being lovingly lowered in temperature to exactly four degrees. Of course, I had to promise my first-born great-grandson in order to take delivery of this miracle of champagnery, but I'm confident it will be worth it. Can I tempt you with a bottle?'

'What say you?' Luc asked Gabrielle. 'Shall we devote the evening to marvelling at the competition?'

'I think we should.'

Paolo rattled off the daily specials before indicating the blackboard menu on the wall and leaving them alone to make their selections.

Gabrielle sat back, and looked around Paolo's restaurant with wide approving eyes.

She smiled and that relaxed Luc. The murmur of contented voices and the aroma of good cooking soothed the beast inside him. The flickering candlelight settled him. The breaking of bread redirected Luc's hunger enough that he could look at Gabrielle without his body screaming for release. She'd turned off the courtesan for the moment and only the real Gabrielle shone through. The one who approved of an old bread vendor aiming high and reaching his goals. The one who'd treated Paolo with the same courtesy and respect one would afford a statesman and had probably never treated him any differently.

Luc had known many beautiful women but he'd never known one with less awareness of her beauty than Gabrielle. Granted, she'd been surrounded by remarkable good looks, what with Rafe for a brother and Josien for a mother, but she'd never seemed to find beauty within herself, never mind that her resemblance to her mother was remarkable.

She didn't see it, thought Luc as he sat back the better to study her face in the candlelight. She just didn't see it.

'What?' she asked him warily. 'I hope you didn't mind me talking to Paolo. He always had a kind word for me. Always.'

'I don't mind you talking to Paolo.'

'Then what is it?'

'Nothing.'

'I'm not seeing nothing.'

Funny that. Because she was probably blind enough. He wondered where a compliment might fit into the grand scheme of things. Simone hadn't said anything about limiting compliments. Besides, he'd done a great deal of talking about puppies already. He was fresh out of pup talk. 'You're beautiful.'

Gabrielle hadn't known exactly how much she'd missed France until she sat in Paolo's tiny crowded restaurant on a Saturday night with Luc. Lulled into relaxation by champagne neither she nor Luc could find fault with, she sat back and set about getting to know the man Luc had become.

He was a sensualist—it showed in the pleasure he took from his food and his surroundings. An intimidating man, she thought, studying his face in the candlelight and finding no softness there. The softness was in her memories of him as a child. They might have called him Night but he hadn't been all brooding and restless darkness. He'd been her knight at times—champion of the underdog. Where had his restlessness gone? she wondered. The recklessness she remembered? Did he still dream of conquering new frontiers or had the challenges that came with being the head of the House of Duvalier been enough for him?

No, they hadn't, she realised with blinding clarity. That was what his fascination with the Hammerschmidt vineyard was all about. He didn't need a crumbling manoir surrounded by a couple of hundred acres of worthless grapevines, no matter how closely located to Caverness they were. He needed a challenge. Beneath all that seemingly effortlessly acquired wealth and charm, a panther paced the cage. Bound by birthright. Fettered by society's expectations. He'd been as trapped by Caverness as she'd been.

He was still trapped. Pacing. Pacing.

That was what drew her to this man so completely. The bone-deep knowledge that when it came to making love with him the panther would escape his cage and be exactly what he was meant to be. As dark as night. As fierce as the devil. And free.

She wanted to be alone with him, wanted it with a fierce and urgent intensity.

He looked at her and he knew her thoughts. No words required.

Never underestimate the power of pheromones.

'How's the food?' she asked.

'Excellent. Yours?'

'Mmm. Exquisite.'

'How am I doing so far?' he murmured. 'Civilised enough for you?' His words held a dark and dangerous edge that made her shudder in anticipation.

'Yes.'

'Ready to bed me now?'

'Yes.' Her body felt boneless, languorous, as the panther rattled the cage.

'Right now and to hell with coffee and dessert?'

'Yes.'

Paolo materialised beside them as if drawn there by the force of Luc's will alone.

'Are you sure?' murmured Luc. Gabrielle nodded. Luc's eyes didn't leave her face. 'Paolo, we'd like the bill.'

Paolo looked at their half eaten meals and the still half-full bottle of precious champagne. 'But is there something wrong?' Luc smiled tightly and a look passed between them. 'Ah,' said the old man. '*Bon appétit*. I will put a regular cork in the Saracenne so you may take it with you.'

'*Non*, Paolo. Take it to the kitchen and do with it what you will. The meal was outstanding, as always. My compliments to you and your family.'

Gabrielle was never sure how she managed to stand and to walk to the door of the restaurant as if everything were not bathed in the colour of desire. She got her coat on with Luc's help and watched with eyes that followed every movement of his long, strong fingers as he did up her buttons and cinched her belt tight.

He reached for her the moment they were seated in the relative privacy of the car, his fingers in her hair, expertly seeking and removing pins as his lips slanted over hers and demanded she open for him. He groaned when she did, the raw and needy groan of a man pushed to his limits as his tongue began a fiercely sensual invasion, stripping her of everything but the need to respond. Her hands went to his hair, she wanted it free, and it took her less than two seconds to achieve that particular goal. Her hair came down more slowly—the hairdresser had been thorough—but when it finally tumbled down around her shoulders and over the lapels of her coat Luc groaned again as the intensity of his kiss ratcheted up another notch. Gabrielle wrenched her lips from his and pushed him away with an unsteady hand.

'Drive,' she ordered raggedly.

'Where?'

'Anywhere.' Although… 'Maybe not Caverness.' Her courage did not extend to flaunting her intimacy with Luc in Josien's face—not because of what her mother might think of her, but because Gabrielle feared that somehow, heaven only knew how, Josien would turn her feelings for Luc into something ugly. 'My room.'

'Caverness is my home, Gabrielle.' His voice was as ragged and strained as hers. 'Sooner or later I will want you there.' But he drove towards the old mill and said no more as they exited the Audi and strode towards the front door. 'I aim to stay the night.'

'I aim to let you.'

Conversation complete.

They met no one on the way to Gabrielle's room. She preceded Luc inside, he locked the door behind him, and she made one last desperate attempt at being civil as she turned to face him and lifted her chin. 'Drink?'

'No.' He shrugged off his coat and tossed it over a chair before coming to stand in front of her, not touching her, not yet. But his eyes promised her every wild thing she wanted of him this night. Everything and more. 'I want you.'

Her hands went to the buckle on her coat and then to the buttons. Moments later a cloud of black leather landed at her feet. She smiled and arched an eyebrow in wordless challenge. 'Which bits?'

'All of them.' A smile crossed his lips, a smile no sensible woman would turn her back on, but she did just that and swept her hair to one side and glanced at him over her shoulder.

'The clasp on my necklace is a little stiff.' Her gaze slid down that lithe and intimidating body and her smile grew the tiniest bit smug. He was ready for her. 'Would you mind? I'd hate to break it.'

His fingers brushed the back of her neck and the necklace came loose in her hand. Luc slid his hands to her shoulders then, his palms warm, cupping the curve of them before he slowly trailed his fingers down her arms. 'You could start with the back of my neck,' she offered. His lips on the bare and sensitive curve of her shoulder.

'I could,' he murmured.

But he didn't.

He started with the zip that ran down the back of her dress, lowering it slowly, smoothly, before walking around her, studying her the way an art aficionado might study a Da Vinci. 'What's underneath?' he said, his voice a husky purr.

'Oh, nothing much.' She wasn't going to step out of her dress for him. If he wanted her undressed he could do it himself. 'I've often wondered what would have happened all those years ago,' she murmured, 'if we hadn't been interrupted. You were sitting on an old wooden table, I believe. As for me...' Her eyes caught Luc's and held. 'I was sitting on you.'

'I'm warning you, Gabrielle. If you want a re-enactment, this is going to get out of control fast.'

'Maybe.' Maybe that was exactly what she wanted. 'There's a table here.'

'There's a *bed* here,' he countered darkly.

Yes, there was. 'Maybe if you sat on the edge of it...'

'Maybe if you let me kiss you...'

That was what he'd said to her last time, too. She stepped forward and offered him her lips, the lightest touch.

'More,' he whispered, and she was catapulted back to the caves of Caverness and she was sixteen and trembling with equal parts terror and lust as she offered Luc more and spun them into madness.

They were on the bed before she knew it, Luc sitting on it with Gabrielle wrapped around him, her knees either side of him, while he devoured her mouth, one hand in her wild tumble of hair and the other on her derrière, urging her closer to his straining hardness. Last time he'd done that, her innocence had left her gasping in shock at his boldness. This time she gasped at the outrageous size of him, the thickness and heat that went on, and on.

Her dress was no barrier to hands as sure as Luc's. His hands were on the rounded globes of her buttocks in an instant, sliding over the silk of her panties as he surged against her. With a ragged moan Gabrielle put her hands to his face as she'd done once before and poured all that she was into a meeting of mouths.

'Would we have managed to take our clothes off, do you think?' she murmured against his lips.

'No,' he whispered as his fingers slid beneath the edge of her panties. 'Maybe some of them. Maybe if I could have got them off you without having to let you go.'

'How?'

The sibilant hiss of shredding silk gave her

an answer she approved of wholeheartedly. She doubted that she would have been bold enough to reach for his belt at sixteen, but she reached for it now in her haste for skin against skin. His zipper went next and then his briefs. She glanced down, measuring him with her eyes, willing her body not to want so badly, willing herself to relax and to wait. 'I'd have been a little nervous right about now. Back then.' Hell, she was a little nervous *now*.

His eyes had darkened, there was fury there, carefully banked. 'I'd have taken care of you.' There was bite in his words. 'I'd not have disappointed you.' Long dark lashes shaded his eyes as he bent his head and set his lips to her collarbone, used his teeth on her there to nip and his tongue to caress. 'Why didn't you wait?'

Ah. There. There was the bite. But she wasn't entirely to blame for bestowing her virginity elsewhere. 'Why didn't you ask me to?' She craved his mouth on her breasts and had no hesitation about twining her hands in his hair and dragging his head there none too gently. Her dress fell away, and she whimpered her satisfaction as she closed her eyes and let sensation ride her, rule her, as her tightly budded nipple made contact with the heat of his tongue and the hardness of teeth.

Lucien could be savage, when he wanted to be. He was savage now, closing his lips over her and suckling hard, darkly pleased by her wild keening cry and the convulsive arch of her body. This wasn't about sex; sex was about bodies. This was possession, and he wanted her soul.

He drew her back on the bed to lay atop him and she went with him willingly, better for her because of his size, better for him because he had access to all of her. Another tremor ripped through her as he suckled her other breast, and with another whimper she settled herself against his length and rocked against him, her body already swollen and slick with need. Her dress had bunched around her waist, and she still wore her shoes but apart from that she was naked. He craved skin on skin, all of her up against every last bit of him. Her dress slid over her head easily; her shoes were harder to get her out of but he managed.

'Shirt,' he muttered, right before her lips claimed his. She undid all of two buttons before haste and frustration got the better of her. Fisting her hands in his shirt, she wrenched it apart. Buttons flew and Luc's breath left his body with a whoosh as she began to trace the curve of muscle over rib, of nipple over muscle. 'Now,' he muttered, with the last of his control. 'Gabrielle, I need to be inside you *now*.' He'd waited so long already. Foreplay and patience were not an option.

'Just so you know,' she muttered as she took him in hand and guided him slowly into her centre. 'I don't want you civilised and gentle. I just want you.'

And just like that, she released the panther from his cage.

He filled her in an instant, rolling her onto her back, fighting for supremacy over her and control of himself as he eased out of her and slid back home. Over and over, while her body destroyed his with greedy hands and a reckless mouth that drove him insane. 'No.' He had to keep control, he had to. He could not lose himself to this.

'More,' she whispered as he eased up on one elbow and splayed his other hand across the softness of her belly and found her centre with his thumb. This time the rhythm he set up was twofold in its intensity and she responded as if he'd taken a whip to her. Straining, clinging, screaming.

He watched her eyes go blind as she crested the peak. He felt convulsions rack her body as she came for him, over and over; she came for him hard.

Then and only then did he allow himself his own release.

Gabrielle lay quietly in the aftermath of Luc's possession, her body not yet recovered enough to do more than breathe, and her mind not functional enough to assess the situation.

'What was that?' she asked finally.

'Overdue,' he said darkly. 'At least, that's what I'm hoping the reason for that particular madness was.' A shudder ripped through him and he twitched inside her, still filling her completely. 'Long, long overdue.'

'Okay.' She pondered the secrets of the universe for a while. Deliberated on what the goddess of lust would have thought of that little display. 'Felt a little intense,' she said next. 'Is that, ah, normal? For you?'

'Yes.'

'Oh.'

'No,' he admitted gruffly.

'Me either. Good though,' she added and

lapsed back into contemplation. 'If that sort of uncontrollable edge thing works for you.'

'Yes.' He rolled onto his back but he did not pull out of her or away from her. He took her with him. He still had his shirt half on, his trousers mostly on. She wasn't wearing a stitch.

'Does it?' She hoped her voice wasn't telegraphing the anxiousness she felt. 'I mean… It could take some getting used to if you're not used to it. If you're a person who likes being in control of things… I mean.'

'Gabrielle?' His hand came up to cradle her skull and his lips brushed her forehead. 'Shut up.'

Shutting up. Shutting right up. Excellent suggestion. 'Luc?'

'What?' His voice sounded long suffering.

'Can we do it again?' The twitch of his body seemed to suggest he could.

'Yes.'

'Soon?'

'Yes.'

'Luc?'

'*What?*'

She shifted to settle astride him, her hands on his bare chest and her thoughts a little grave. 'I know I still have to figure out how to remove the bulk of your clothes without giving up my position of dominance here, but do you think that this time you could be naked too?'

She got him naked. She got him sweaty. She got his hands fisted above his head as he poured his release into her and cried out her name.

But she could not, until that very last moment, make him surrender himself to her completely.

CHAPTER EIGHT

THE stone-faced miller's wife lasted all of ten minutes after Luc left the following morning before rapping on the door and informing Gabrielle that the room had been re-let and that she would need to find accommodation elsewhere. Today. Oh, and she had thirty minutes to pack.

This time, Gabrielle took a three-month lease on a fully furnished apartment situated on a leafy square in the expensive part of town.

If anyone tried to kick her out of this place for being lover to a single man of good standing, she'd damn well go out and buy a house. No one was going to belittle the rapture she'd found in Luc's arms.

No one.

Simone, bless her, did not even try. She came round for coffee at Gabrielle's new abode, her smile warm and her treatment of Gabrielle exactly the same. A little confrontation, a lot of teasing, and always the underlying warmth of a sister of the heart. She did not repeat her warning of yesterday. Now that the deed with Luc had been done, Simone accepted it with the ease of one well used to accommodating life's little inconsistencies.

'Nice,' said Simone after looking through the apartment. 'But why the sudden change? I thought you had a few more days before your time at the old mill was up?'

'I needed something with a little more room,' said Gabrielle. 'And I needed it now.'

'She threw you out, didn't she?' Simone's gaze was very direct.

'Yes.'

'Because Luc stayed over?'

'Not in so many words, but yes. I think so.'

'Does Luc know?'

'No, and I'd appreciate it if you didn't mention it to him. I needed more space so I moved. End of story.'

'It's a good story, don't get me wrong,' said Simone. 'Let's just pray Luc never hears the other one.'

'Amen,' said Gabrielle.

'So, who won the war?' asked Simone next.

'Not me and stop prying. We are not having this conversation.'

'Just trying to keep up with the situation to hand,' said Simone. And with an impish grin. 'You don't look like a casualty of war.'

'I'm not.' Not yet, at any rate. 'And I really can't talk to you about this, Simone. It's too new. I don't even understand what's going on myself yet.'

'So who will you talk to about it?' asked Simone. 'Will you tell Rafe?'

'Not yet.'

'Because it's too new or because you know he won't like it?'

Gabrielle smiled wryly. 'Both.'

'Will you tell Josien?'

'No,' she said, her smile fading fast. 'That door is closed to me, Simone, and I'm done with standing on one side of it like a needy child waiting for it to open. There's nothing for me there.' Nothing but pain. 'Nothing there for Rafael either.'

'Gabrielle—' Simone's expression grew sombre. '*Maman* died so long ago I can hardly remember her, but I never envied you yours. I know she made childhood difficult for you. I wish things could have been different for you. For you and Rafe both.'

'Me too.'

'I know she used to hit you.' Simone hesitated, not quite managing to meet Gabrielle's gaze. 'I saw her once. Not smacking you. Not scolding you for whatever it was she thought you'd done wrong. She was beating you. Hurting you.' Simone shook her head as if to deny the memory of it. 'I ran for my father but by the time we returned you were gone. My father said he'd talk to Josien but talking isn't doing, so I went and found Rafael and told him what I'd seen. I'll never forget the look on his face, Gaby. The helpless fury in his eyes. The pain and the fear. He was twelve and you were six and I knew at once that this wasn't the first time she'd hurt you. We ran back to the chateau and Rafe told me to go inside, and that he would find you and take care of you, and I went inside because I was scared. Gabrielle, I'm so sorry I never did anything. Not then. Not later, when Rafe would treat you with such care and tenderness that I knew in my heart she had taken to you again.' Simone looked tortured. 'Did he find you?'

'Always,' said Gabrielle with a tiny smile. 'Always.' She covered Simone's hands with her own and willed Simone to look at her. 'You were a child too, Simone. You did what you could. Your father did what he could— he made Josien seek counselling for her anger and her rage and it helped. It helped a lot. Besides, you forget that I was no angel. Sometimes I deserved to be punished.'

'Not like that,' said Simone fiercely. 'Never like that, and not later either when she came at you with words rather than whips. Don't let her hurt you again, Gaby. Don't you listen to her when she tells you that what you've found with my brother is wrong. Don't let anyone tell you that!'

'I won't.' But the weight of Simone's words settled heavily on Gabrielle's mind. Reminding her, as if she needed reminding, that not everyone would see her relationship with Luc in a positive light. Josien would disapprove. Rafe, with his uncomfortable history with Simone, would wish she'd chosen differently. And then there was the yawning social and economic gulf between a man of Luc's standing and a woman like herself. Gabrielle tried to feel worthy of Luc but she was desperately vulnerable to the judgement of others. She was a product of her childhood, of Josien's beliefs about class and about status, and those lessons learned early were not so easily disregarded. There was truth in them, and sense in them, no matter how much she wished otherwise. 'I'm feeling morose.'

'Likewise,' said Simone. 'You have no idea how I worried for you as a child.'

Gabrielle turned away, carefully, casually. 'Did Luc know?'

'That Josien used to beat you? No,' said Simone faintly. 'He suspected, but no one ever confirmed his suspicions. Not Rafe. Not you. And certainly not me. Rafe was so very level-headed about it, you see? Whereas Luc…' Simone shook her head again, more memories denied. 'Luc would not have kept a level head at all. So we protected you, as best we could. We shielded Luc from the ugliness you endured at your mother's hands, and I prayed to God every night that I was doing the right thing.'

'From where I'm standing, you did exactly the right thing. Look at me, Simone, and tell me what you see. Am I damaged? Am I fearful or abusive? Do I look upon love and the giving of it as a weakness or a curse? No. I think I turned out just fine. I think all of the children of Caverness turned out fine.

The occasional minor flaw here and there, maybe…' She thought of Rafe's compulsion to succeed. Of the fierce need the children of Caverness had to protect each other, even now, so many years later. 'Probably. But who doesn't have those? I'm fine. And you…' Gabrielle smiled and reached for Simone's hand, seeking strength in touch and finding it. 'Such a valiant and tender heart. It's no surprise that my brother cannot forget you. The surprise is that he's stayed away from you this long.'

'Well, when you put it that way,' said Simone with a choked laugh, 'you're absolutely right. The man's a fool and I'm a goddess. I could grow quite fond of this perspective.'

'Keep it,' said Gabrielle with a squeeze of her hand. 'Embrace it.'

'Maybe I will,' said Simone. 'Mind you, I'm still going to need chocolate in order to get over all this soul-baring and childhood trauma.'

'Chocolate would help,' agreed Gabrielle thoughtfully. 'Belgian?'

'Oh, Gaby.' Simone's laughter came more freely this time. 'Is there any other kind?'

Two days and two Luc-filled nights later, and midway through their rapidly developing morning ritual of showering and having breakfast together before getting on with their respective workloads, Luc confronted her about her reluctance to dine with him that evening at Caverness. It was a conversation Gabrielle had seen coming. It wasn't one she particularly wanted to have.

'I'm not ashamed that we're lovers, Gabrielle,' he said, his expression tightly controlled as he pulled a clean shirt from his overnight bag and shoved his arms through the sleeves. 'Why are you?'

'I'm not,' she said defensively, a damp towel wrapped securely around her as she rummaged through the wardrobe for something to wear. 'I'm just uncomfortable about going to Caverness with Josien there, that's all.' There, she'd said it.

'She can hardly bring herself to even acknowledge you, Gabrielle,' said Luc bluntly. 'What makes you think she'll give a damn?'

'She probably won't,' muttered Gabrielle, shielding her distress from Luc behind an open cupboard door. 'But it'd be like handing her a weapon, and I do know what she does with those.'

And then Luc's hands were on her shoulders, gently turning her around to face him. 'I won't let her hurt you,' he said quietly.

'Luc…' Gabrielle tried to think of a way to convey her fears without provoking the warrior in him. 'This isn't your fight, it's mine and I just don't want to set her off again.'

'I'll stop her,' said Luc. 'Trust me.'

But in this she could not. 'You know what she said to me last time?' she said with the bracing of her shoulders and the clenching of her heart. 'She said that Harrison wasn't Rafe's father.'

Luc stilled, every inch of his big body radiating tension. 'Did she tell you who was?'

'No.' Gabrielle's lips twisted. 'My guess is she's saving that little snippet for the moment where it will do the most damage. How can I look at her after that, Luc? How can I look at her and not hate her?' Luc stared at her in silence, his expression guarded but not surprised. It was his lack of surprise, the swift calculation behind his gaze before he offered up a response, that caused her to step back swiftly, away from his touch. 'You know.' Her hands shook, everything shook. 'You know who Rafe's father is.'

Luc inclined his head warily.

'Who?' Gabrielle clenched her arms

tightly around her middle. 'Lucien, who?' Dear God, not Phillipe. That would make Rafe half-brother to Lucien, half brother to Simone, and that would destroy him. Him and Simone both. She shook her head. 'No. No, it *can't* be.' She couldn't hold Luc's gaze. 'Not Phillipe.'

'It's not Phillipe,' said Luc immediately. 'God, no! Is that what you thought?'

'I didn't know what to think! She gave me half the story, Luc. The only man I've ever known who was able to reason with Josien was your father. The only man ever to put up with her moods was your father! What was I supposed to think?'

'It wasn't Phillipe,' said Luc. 'Gabrielle, no! Rafe's father was a guest here at Caverness. A friend of my father's who came to stay for the summer the year your mother turned sixteen. A man well used to taking what he wanted. A prince.'

'He *raped* her? This *prince* amongst men?'

'No.' Luc smiled grimly. 'Your mother fell in love with him. And he with her, at least for a little while. Until she fell pregnant. He would not marry her, Gabrielle. He could not. His marriage had already been arranged.'

'To a princess, no doubt.'

'That bit I don't know.'

Gabrielle's initial fury that Luc had known all along what she didn't was gone, washed away in the relief that Phillipe was not Rafael's father. But cold, hard anger remained and found a target in Luc. 'So how do you know what you do know? Why you and no one else?'

'My father told me before he died. He felt responsible for Josien's circumstances to some extent. Responsible for Rafael's upbringing, and yours too for that matter. He had assured the prince that Josien and her child would always have a home at Caverness. He wanted to make sure I would not renege on his words.'

'He did *what*?'

'He did what he could,' said Luc. 'Surely you can see that? My father wasn't always right. He wasn't often there, for that matter. But he was honourable, and he did what he could to improve your mother's lot.'

'I—' Gabrielle stared at him, barely taking in the words. 'Oh, damn.' It explained so much about her mother's attitude and her actions, her biases and her rage. Why Josien had never had any time or love for Rafael.

Why Gabrielle had been shipped off so rapidly after Josien had found her and Luc together. 'So it's true. You have no idea how badly I didn't want it to be true.' What was she supposed to *do* with this information? 'Does Rafe know?'

'I've never told him,' said Luc.

Then he didn't know. Rafael thought Harrison Alexander was his father. 'Does Simone know?'

'No. At least, I think not. Again, I've never told her,' said Luc gruffly. 'I've never told anyone, Gabrielle. Until now.'

'Thank you.' With her arms still tightly clasped around her waist, Gabrielle tried a smile but couldn't keep it on her face. Rafael was only her half-brother and the bastard son of some lousy prince who'd once had a penchant for seducing sixteen-year-old girls. Rafe would love that. 'What do I tell him?' she whispered. 'What do I tell Rafe?'

'If you want my advice, nothing,' said Luc. 'This isn't your secret to tell, Gabrielle. This is between Josien and Rafe.'

'So why did she go and tell *me*?'

Luc sighed heavily. 'My guess is that you were right. She wanted to wound you, and what better way than by trying to take away from you the one person who's always been there for you? She wants you gone, Gabrielle. You threaten her. You always have.'

'I threaten nothing!'

'She sees herself in you: a class-locked woman about to take up with a wealthy man who'll doubtless discard you after the fascination fades. She sees no other course for you.'

'She's wrong,' said Gabrielle in a low and shaking voice. 'I have *many* options open to me.'

'Happens I think so too,' murmured Luc. 'She can't win this battle, Gabrielle. She can't take Rafe away from you and she can't make me stay away from you either. Not this time. Not unless you let her. Come to Caverness with me tonight. Stay for dinner. Stay the night. Fight her. Don't you dare let her win.'

'I won't.' She was not like her mother. She refused to be. 'I'll come to Caverness with you.' While the fear of not being strong enough to withstand yet another of Josien's vicious assaults wrapped around her like a suffocating and blinding fog.

'And you'll stay the night in my bed?'

'Yes.'

Luc crossed to her and took her in his arms and she let him, absorbing his strength and his certainty. She would need it for the night ahead. He smiled his encouragement and his lips brushed hers. A promise wrapped in a kiss. 'That's my girl.'

The evening started well as far as Luc was concerned. Josien was resting in her rooms and did not require visitors. Hans saw to Josien's meal. Luc saw to everyone else's. Simone saw Gabrielle's unease and tried to put it to rest with easy talk about nothing much, and Gabrielle tried to settle and follow Simone's lead; she really gave it a solid shot.

But she jumped six feet when Luc settled down to watch television beside her, and she did not snuggle up beside him as had become her habit. Gabrielle did not look out of place to Luc's eyes, but he could tell from looking into her eyes that she was finding the entire experience acutely uncomfortable.

Behind the mask of self-assured lover lay the heart of the housekeeper's daughter and she saw no place for herself here, and Luc could think of no other way to ease her anxiety than to take her to his room and within their lovemaking make the world around them disappear, at least for a little while.

Simone yawned loudly after the end of her favourite show, pleading tiredness before swooping down to give Gabrielle a kiss on each cheek before doing the same to Luc. 'Come with me into Epernay in the morning if you feel like it,' she offered to Gabrielle. 'I'll show you what I do. Lucien, may I see you for a moment?'

Luc followed his sister into the hallway, wary for no reason he could fully comprehend other than he thought he was in trouble and he couldn't figure out why.

'What are you *doing*?' she said when she judged them far enough away that Gabrielle could not hear their words.

'What do you mean?'

'Gabrielle's wound so tight you could snap her with a glance.'

'Yes, thank you. I had noticed.'

'Well, *do* something.'

'Do what? Tell her to stop feeling like she doesn't belong here? It doesn't work that way, Simone. Gabrielle has to fight that particular battle herself.'

'It'd help if you got rid of Josien,' muttered Simone. 'She's a good housekeeper, Lucien, but can't you see that this won't work? You can't have the housekeeper's estranged daughter in your life as your mistress and expect *anyone* to feel comfortable. If you want Gabrielle in your life—and clearly you do—Josien and her intolerance will have to find a place out of it.'

Luc shoved a hand through his hair, cursing the promise he'd made to a dying old man. 'Josien stays,' he said curtly.

'But *why*? You don't like her, Luc. You tolerate her. We both do. As for Gabrielle...Gabrielle's afraid of her and with good cause. Can't you see that it's time we let her go?'

'Josien stays,' he said tightly. 'I promised Phillipe she would always have a home here.'

'Why would he demand such a promise of you?' Simone's eyes grew even more troubled. 'I know he acted like the king of the damn castle at times, but Josien's not an in-dentured serf and it's not our duty to look after her for the rest of her life, or ours. Give her a job in one of our other offices if you must. Send her to Paris, make her a House of Duvalier sales rep and watch her slay the competition. Ask her if she's ever considered doing something other than keeping house at

Caverness and, if she has, make it happen for her. I don't care what it takes, Lucien, just get her *away* from here. Because this thing you have with Gabrielle won't work until you do.'

'She's right,' said a voice from the shadows. Josien's voice. Luc turned and there she stood in the doorway to the library, looking tragically beautiful and disturbingly frail. Hans stood behind her, a silent, watchful presence.

Simone groaned, but then she rallied. Luc watched as Simone's eyes grew hard and completely without mercy, harder than he'd ever seen them. '*Have* you ever considered doing something else for a living, Josien?' Woman to woman and smothered in ice. Luc's gaze met Hans', the older man lifted his hands in surrender. Not buying in. But Luc had to. Simone had left him no choice.

'There is an opening in the Paris office for a sales rep,' he offered carefully. 'We also have an apartment there that you could use until you found your feet.' He wasn't reneging on his father's promise. Surely he wasn't. 'You could go to Paris once you're more fully recovered and take a look at both the accommodation and the position on offer.'

'I could drive you.' Hans stepped forward and offered his arm to Josien with a gentle smile. 'Make sure you did not overtax yourself. I've never seen Paris in the spring-time. Have you?'

Josien stared at Hans, her eyes wide and uncertain, and then she did something that Luc had never seen her do. She blushed. 'No,' she said quietly. 'I have not.'

'So, you're interested?' said Simone, her eyes still flinty, every inch the autocratic mistress of the house. A mistress who'd had more than enough of this particular employee's presence. 'You'll look at taking a position elsewhere?'

'Yes,' said Josien.

Luc returned to the lounge room with a lighter step than when he'd left it. Gabrielle wasn't on the sofa where he'd left her. She was pacing the room restlessly, every movement of that lithe and lovely body poised as if to run.

'No,' he said.

'You haven't even heard what I'm going to say.'

'No, it would not be better if you left. It would be infinitely worse. So stay.' He shot her a knowing stare. 'How am I doing so far?'

'So-so,' she said grudgingly.

'So will you stay?'

A tiny smile lifted her lips. 'I'll need incentive.'

'I'll be sure to provide it.'

'A little privacy…'

'My room is very private. So private it's positively remote. Matter of fact I'm heading there now.'

'What else is in this room of yours?'

'A bed,' he said. 'Good mattress. Four posts. You'll like it.'

Her smile grew a little more sure but her eyes stayed uncertain. 'I don't know why I'm so worried about being here with you like this. I just am. It was different at my place. More neutral and less complicated, whereas when we come here…' She shrugged awkwardly. 'All the stuff that's happened between us in the past comes crashing on in. It's not just you and me any more—it's Simone and Rafe and Josien as well, and how what we're doing affects them.'

'I know.' He took her in his arms. 'Has anyone ever told you that you think too much?'

'No.'

'Well, you do. Fortunately, I have a solution. Come to bed with me. Now. I guarantee I can turn your mind to something that doesn't require any thought at all.'

Her smile turned wry, but she hooked her arms around his neck and brushed her lips across his. 'Has anyone ever told you that you have an extremely one track mind?'

'No, but I am aware of it,' he countered with a grin.

It took them for ever to reach Luc's bedroom. He needed to kiss her halfway up the stairs and again at the top of them. Two steps later he cornered her against the wall, just past the gilt-edged mirror, and laid waste to her hairpins before ravishing her neck. His knees almost buckled when he pushed her up against doorway to his study and she wrapped her legs around his waist and dragged his mouth to her breast. He managed to get the door closed behind them, managed to carry her to the big brown leather sofa and deposit her on it before his hunger got the better of him and he pushed her skirt waistwards and, kneeling, set his lips to the soft and creamy skin of her inner thighs.

'You'll let me know if there's anything

else bothering you, won't you?' he muttered as he wrapped his hands around her buttocks, dragged her closer, and set himself the task of reaching his final destination some time this decade.

Gabrielle whimpered and twined her hands in his hair, muscles quivering and her eyes dark with desire as she stared down at him. 'Yes, I'll let you know.'

'Like if you'd rather watch something else on television.'

'Okay.'

He brushed the inside of her knee with his lips. 'Or if you'd rather have something else for dinner.'

Her hands tightened in his hair. 'Yes. Yes, I'll let you know.' She sounded distracted. She *was* distracted.

He dragged his lips along her inner thigh. 'What kind of toothpaste do you use?' he murmured, and grazed her skin with his teeth.

'Oh, hell,' she muttered.

'Not sure I know that one but I'll do my best. You know me.' Very deliberately he brushed his knuckles over her panties, sliding his lips a little closer to his goal when she whimpered again and opened her thighs wider for him. 'I like to fix things.'

'Luc…' She strained against him, already lost to sensation, already at the mercy of her body's response to him. He loved that about her, that she could give herself over to him so completely during lovemaking. Loved it, and feared it because one day, some day, he would follow her, and once he did that would be it for him. There would be no other women— no other love for him—but Gabrielle.

He feared losing himself to her.

He feared he could become utterly obsessed with her.

He feared he already was.

'Luc, please!'

'Tell me what you want.'

'You. I want you.'

'Where?' His teeth scraped the edge of her panties.

'Everywhere.'

'Hold on,' he murmured and, pushing her panties aside, set his mouth to her in earnest.

She held on for less than a minute before her first climax overtook her. He freed himself and plunged inside her moments after that, holding on, holding on so very tightly to his control as he drove her to climax again, and again, until finally his screams joined her own.

* * *

Luc seemed a little withdrawn at breakfast the following morning, at least as far as Gabrielle was concerned. They'd spent most of the night in each other's arms, making love or making war, Gabrielle never quite knew which one it was—all she knew was that when it was over her body was boneless and her mind was blissfully blank.

Whatever was running through Luc's mind at those times was a mystery to her.

For all his teasing words in the lead up to their lovemaking, Luc never had much to say in the aftermath. He held her, that was all. He held her close and kept his thoughts to himself.

Simone had left for work not long ago, obviously having realized Gabrielle wasn't going to be ready in time to go with her. Josien and Hans were nowhere to be seen. She and Luc were here alone. She should have been relaxed. *Luc* should have been relaxed.

He wasn't.

'I'm sensing a little discomfort here,' she said as he attempted to disappear inside the morning paper. 'Have I overstayed my welcome?'

He lowered the paper carefully, a picture of elegance and control. 'No.'

'Then talk to me.'

'About what?'

'*Anything*. Something. Tell me what your plans are for the day and I'll tell you mine. Ask me what I thought of our lovemaking last night. Tell me what you thought of it.'

'I thought…' He set the paper down completely, ran his hands through his hair and looked towards the window. 'I thought that if our lovemaking had been any more perfect I'd have died from need of you,' he said quietly. 'I thought, when I thought at all, that a man would have to be mad not to want to wake up to you every day, and I wondered what the hell I'd do when next I didn't.' His gaze cut back to hers, guarded and strangely angry. 'Is that enough of my thoughts for you, Gabrielle? Do you want more?'

'I, ah, no.' There seemed to be plenty to be going on with there. 'So we, ah, take a lot of pleasure in being with each other. This is a good thing.' She tried a tentative smile. 'Isn't it?'

He stared at her broodingly. 'So what did *you* think of last night?'

'I thought…' She had the insane urge to be utterly truthful, to lay herself bare with her words as well as her body. 'I thought that if I gave any more of myself to you there'd be nothing left for me.' She met his gaze head-on. 'Does that help any?'

'Not in the slightest,' he said gruffly, and, leaning across the table, captured her lips with his. 'What are your plans for the day?'

'I'm inspecting some wine storage facilities at one of the vineyards first up, then I have a meeting with a distributor in Epernay who's interested enough in the Angels Landing reds to give me twenty minutes of his time—this is, by the way, a major coup. And then I'm meeting with the Hammerschmidt vineyard estate agent to get some chemical use history and soil and water test information, and quiz him about whether there are any restoration restrictions on the house.'

'You do know you could get all the Hammerschmidt information directly from me and save yourself that particular part of your day?' he murmured.

'Yes, but then the agent would not know who I was and that might prove a problem if I want to bid for the property at auction,' she whispered back amidst kisses.

'And do you?'

'I do. Rafe, on the other hand, needs a little more convincing.'

'It's a big investment, Gabrielle, and the place has a lot of drawbacks.'

'Do you plan to bid on it?'

'Up to a point,' he said, and moved his lips to the curve of her jaw. 'The purchase needs to be an economically smart move for the House of Duvalier. As soon as the price goes above twenty million, the bidding is over for me.'

'Just like that?' she said.

'Yes.' His mouth continued to wreak havoc with the nerves beneath her ear. 'Just like that. If your calculations stack up better than mine and you're prepared to pay more, it's yours. No hard feelings.'

Gabrielle closed her eyes, wound her hands in his hair, and tried to continue the conversation without whimpering. 'I'm not sure my calculations are going to get me above that price. For us, there's also the thought that a twenty-million-euro outlay will buy us a lot more vineyard in Australia than it will over here. That's Rafe's argument.'

'It's a good one,' said Luc.

'I knew you'd say that.' She was in his lap, he was on the chair, and her body was telling her she wanted this man again.

'Unless you have it in mind to try and get

the land rezoned so you can subdivide and sell off part of it, that old vineyard is a lot more land than you need, Gabrielle. A lot more *hassle* than you need.' His hands were on the buttons of her shirt. Hers were on his.

'You know, you sound just like him.' Gabrielle eyed him suspiciously. 'Have you and Rafe been communing by bat phone again?'

'No.' Luc shook his head and his hands stilled. 'I like what you and your brother have built with the Angels Landing wines, Gabrielle. I respect your plans to expand into the European market. But from a purely business perspective there are other ways to achieve the same result. You'd be far better off hooking into someone else's storage and distribution facilities for a while and building your brand before committing to such a large outlay.'

'I know,' she said. It felt good to talk this over with Luc, even if they were potentially vying for the same piece of land. 'I guess I just liked the old place. Nothing to do with business, I know, but it had a nice feel about it. It felt right.' She set her hands to Luc's bare chest and shuddered at the pleasure the contact afforded her. 'Try running that one past Rafe.'

'If you did purchase Hammerschmidt would Rafe return and make it a viable vineyard?'

'Rafe won't return,' said Gabrielle. 'Not to live. He'd definitely want it viable but he loves Australia. He's accepted there. Harrison—' Gabrielle took a deep breath '—Rafe's father gives him a lot of support. Harrison owns grazing property rather than vineyards but he's thrilled by Rafe's progress. He takes an interest. He holds a stake in the business. They get along well.'

'Would Harrison consider a move to Hammerschmidt to oversee the vineyard's renewal?'

Gabrielle hadn't considered that option before. 'He might, but again he has his own properties to run. There's really only me. I've worked alongside Rafe for seven years, Luc. You don't think I could bring that old vineyard back to life?'

'Could you?'

'Yes. With guidance I dare say I could. Although probably not as quickly as you could. I'd have to do it in stages. Buying the place would clean us out. There'd be very little money left for renovation.'

'You'd live in the house?'

'I'd reclaim some of the house, to start

with, so I could live in it. As for the rest…I really don't know what I'd do with the rest.'

'You're not alone there,' he said wryly. 'I haven't quite figured out what use the house would be to me either. Perhaps for Simone…perhaps we need to consider who would live where if one of us ever married.'

Gabrielle's hands stilled along with the rest of her body. He felt her sudden tension, damned if he didn't. 'Is that likely in the near future?'

'I don't know,' he murmured, lifting his gaze from her body to her face, his eyes intent and his face carefully composed. 'Is it?'

'What do you mean?' Gabrielle shied away from the notion that Luc was considering her for marriage. She didn't want the role or the duties that went with it. She only wanted Luc. 'Are you asking me if I would want to live here as your wife?'

'Would you?' he said quietly. 'Could you be comfortable living here as my wife?'

With Josien as housekeeper? With the pressure to fit into the upper echelons of society here? She, the lowly housekeeper's daughter? 'No,' she said raggedly. 'Not without a lot of adjustments that I'm not sure

I have the ability to make. I can be your lover, Lucien. But I wouldn't make you a good wife.'

'Why not? Because you don't want to be or because you think others wouldn't like it?' He didn't sound angry, more curious.

'It's complicated,' she said.

'Not that complicated,' he countered. 'You know the chateau and you know the House of Duvalier business.'

'From the point of view of a child,' she reminded him. 'The child of a servant.'

'Employee,' he said curtly. 'Josien's an employee. Yes, she retreated to Caverness with two young children in tow when her marriage to Harrison didn't work out. Yes, she took on the role of housekeeper, but even then I wonder if she didn't play the part to spite her prince more than anything else. She knows more about society protocols and the smooth running of a chateau than any princess I know. She's been offered more domestic management positions than I can count. Men have tried to court her—rich and poor and titled as well. She owns three apartments that I know of—a small one here in the village and two luxury apartments in Epernay. Josien's an independently wealthy woman in her own right, Gabrielle. She could step into any part of society whenever she wanted to, just like that,' he said with the click of his fingers. 'And so could you.'

'But…' Gabrielle reeled beneath the barrage of information contained in Luc's statement '…why does she stay?'

'Because it suits her,' said Luc with a shrug. 'When it no longer suits her I dare say she'll move on. I've offered Josien a sales position in the Paris office, Gabrielle. I offered it to her last night, with Simone's encouragement. Simone thought—*we* thought—you might be more comfortable around here with Josien gone.'

'Oh.' Gabrielle put the heels of her hands to her eyes, grateful for the darkness, that small reprieve from the bombardment of information that her brain would have to process. Not sight, not right now. Not colour or the wary look on Luc's face as he told her what he and Simone had done. 'You fired her? Because of me?'

'Not fired her. Encouraged her to consider the many options open to a woman of her abilities. And, yes, because of you. She hurts you, Gabrielle. And I won't have it. Not in my house.'

'Oh, Luc.'

'I did warn her,' he said. 'Look at me, Gabrielle. Tell me I'm not a fool for thinking you'd be more comfortable here without Josien around.'

She lowered her hands to his shoulders and raised her gaze to his. 'You're not a fool,' she said. 'Part of me's horrified that you're encouraging Josien to move on because of me. Part of me thinks this could have been avoided altogether if only I'd stayed away from Caverness and from you. I could have stayed away from Caverness, and happily,' she confessed. 'I don't know that I could have stayed away from you.'

'Stay with me again tonight,' he murmured. 'Come over after you finish your work. We can go out to dinner. We can go anywhere you like. Just…be with me.'

'I can do that,' she said as his hand came up to cradle her head.

'Humour me,' he said when next he broke their kiss.

'What do you think I'm doing?' He kissed her again and need roared through her. Would this hunger for him never ease?

'Make love with me,' he whispered, and proceeded to show her exactly how he liked that done.

* * *

Another week passed. A week in which Gabrielle worked hard on putting a fledgling distribution network together that might support her admittedly crazy plans for purchasing the Hammerschmidt vineyard. Rafe had Angels Landing, Luc had Caverness, Simone had…many things she could call her own although Gabrielle couldn't think of anything specific. Even Josien owned residential property. Gabrielle wanted a place to call home too. Not Angels Landing, not Caverness, somewhere else. A place that beckoned to her, somewhere she could fill with new memories and her own belongings. A place where a woman could stare out a window and smile and plan and dream big dreams.

Somewhere like Hammerschmidt.

The auction was tomorrow. She could almost justify, on paper, a purchase bid slightly higher than Luc's. All she had to do was convince Rafe that it was a good idea.

Damn, but she hated making late night pleading phone calls. And tonight she intended to make not one, but two.

It was mid-morning in Australia and Rafe was working. He sounded good humoured. He'd been working in amongst his barrels of wine, he told her. An activity that never failed to lift his spirits.

'Did you get the latest figures I sent you?' she said.

'I got them.'

'Did you go over them?'

'Yes.'

'What do you think?'

'I think you want to bid on the Hammer-schmidt place,' he said dryly. 'And I still think it's unnecessary.'

'From a business perspective, maybe. Probably. I know it's risky, Rafe, but if we got it at the right price it would be a good investment. A good base for European operations. I'd like to bid for it.'

'You've fallen in love with it,' said Rafe heavily.

'Yes.'

'Do you know if anyone else is interested in it?' said Rafe.

'I know that Luc plans to bid for it.'

Silence at that, and then a heavy sigh. 'He'll have more money to throw at it, Gabrielle. You *know* this.'

'I know. We've talked about it a bit. There's no animosity between Luc and I on this, Rafe. We've looked at the place together, talked about what whoever buys it might do with it. A lot of the ideas I sent you about the phased redevelopment of the property came from Luc.'

'Remind me again why he's helping you if he plans to bid for the property himself,' said Rafael curtly.

'Because he wants to,' replied Gabrielle defensively. 'He likes running the different scenarios. I think he sees it as a challenge.'

'Would Luc redevelop the vineyard in stages too?'

'No, he'd do it all at once.'

'Gabrielle…' Rafe paused as if he wasn't quite sure what he wanted to ask. 'Just how much time have you been spending with Luc?'

'A bit.' Gabrielle grimaced and shut her eyes tight. She never had been any good at lying. 'A lot.'

'Are you sleeping with him?'

'We don't really sleep all that much.'

Silence at that and another heavy sigh. 'So you're sleeping with him, planning to bid against him tomorrow for a property you both want, and presumably you intend to continue sleeping with him after that?'

'Yes,' she said warily. 'Something wrong with that?'

Rafe snorted. 'I guess not.' And with

concern rippling through his voice, 'You're playing with fire, Gabrielle.'

'I know,' she said in a small voice. 'Luc's told me his stop bid.' She breathed in deep, gathered her courage, and gave it to him straight. 'It's twenty million. Can we afford to pay more than twenty million?'

More silence. Gabrielle pictured her brother pacing away his frustration, his blue eyes razor sharp and his golden hair glinting in the half light of the cellars. 'I ran your business plan past Harrison,' said Rafe. Rafe didn't sound happy, he sounded resigned. 'We can afford the twenty million but only just. Not without risking Angels Landing, and not without Harrison taking a stake in it. I want you on the phone to me when the bidding commences.'

'You'll be asleep.'

'Trust me,' he said grimly. 'I'll be awake for this. I want your promise that when I say stop, you'll stop.'

'I promise,' she said.

'No matter who's bidding,' he said. 'No matter how close you think they are to their limit price.'

'Got it.'

'No matter how much you want this vineyard.'

'I promise,' she said again. 'On my soul, Rafe. I promise to stop bidding the moment you give the word.'

'All right,' he said. 'On your soul and mine, let's try and bring this one home.'

Gabrielle's next phone call was to Lucien. He'd gone to his Paris offices for the day. He sounded tired and somewhat tetchy. She didn't know if he was home yet, but he hadn't called her and he hadn't come over.

'I'm in my office at Caverness,' he said when she got hold of him. 'And I have your mother and Hans with me.'

Oh. 'Are you on speaker phone?'

'No.' Just a general warning that he wouldn't be talking to her freely, then.

'So if I started talking dirty to you…'

'You would definitely live to regret it.'

'Are you coming over later?' she asked him.

'It'll be late,' he said. 'I've work to finish up first.'

'I don't mind late.'

'You could always come here,' he said quietly. With her mother and Hans sitting beside him and doubtless listening to every word he uttered.

'I—I'd rather not. Not tonight.' While a little voice inside her berated her for being a coward.

'Your place, then,' he said as if it didn't matter. It was the same conversation they had every night, albeit phrased a little differently. His place or hers, as long as he could sleep with her and wake to her. 'Your mother has some news.'

'Am I going to like this news?'

'Here, I'll put her on.'

'No! Luc—' Too late. 'Hello?'

'*Bonjour* Gabrielle.'

'*Maman,*' she said carefully. And waited.

'Luc's been telling me of your plans to stay in the area.'

'Oh.' Had he?

'And of your plans for the old Hammer-schmidt vineyard should your bid tomorrow be successful.'

'Oh.'

'I just wanted to wish you luck,' said Josien. She sounded as if she meant it. 'And to let you know that Hans has accepted a permanent position with an elderly widow in the south of France. She's frail and in need of care.' There was a long pause. 'She's in need of a housekeeper too. Perhaps the position will be filled by the time I'm ready to return to work, perhaps I won't be interested in taking on another housekeeping position, I'm really not sure of my plans just yet but the fact remains that Hans has invited me to go there with him and I've accepted his offer.'

'Oh.' Gabrielle didn't quite know which bombshell she should respond to first. That Josien was leaving Duvalier employ or that she and Hans had decided to move on together. 'I wish you every happiness,' she said finally. 'Whatever you decide to do.'

'I—thank you,' said Josien quietly. 'I would like—if you wouldn't mind—I would like to see you tomorrow morning before the auction. I moved out of the chateau proper and back into my own quarters yesterday. So it would mean that you would come there. For breakfast perhaps, or a mid-morning coffee? Shall we say ten o clock?'

Clamping down hard on her fear of all the hurtful things Josien might have to say to her, Gabrielle said yes.

Luc came to her later that evening, looking weary and stern, and ever so slightly dishevelled. But his eyes lit up when he saw that she'd prepared a supper for him and he wasted no time in devouring it and then reaching for her. He made love to her lazily, expertly bringing her to orgasm before surrendering to his own. These past two weeks of being with him every night had taken some of the urgency away from their lovemaking but none of the passion and sensuality. Luc could make her yearn for him, soar for him, weep for just that little bit more of him.

Even when he held her and kissed her as if the world could crumble around them before he'd ever let her go.

'Luc, may I ask you a question?' she said, propping herself up beside him and letting her eyes feast on the tumbled beauty of the man in her bed.

'Of course,' he murmured, smiling at her with sleepy eyes.

'Why are you always so careful of me when we make love?'

Not the kind of question he'd been expecting. Wariness crept into his eyes as the sleepiness left them. Not the kind of question he looked as if he wanted to answer. 'You'd rather I wasn't?'

'Maybe,' she murmured. 'Maybe I simply want to know why you refuse to let passion rule you completely when you're with me. I worry that you think I wouldn't be able to cope with whatever lies beneath all that iron control. The thing is, I would cope. I'd probably die of ecstasy if you ever truly let abandon take hold of you while you were taking hold of me. So all I'm saying…what I mean to say…is that there's no need to hold back on my account.'

Luc's arm didn't move from its place around her shoulder but she felt the withdrawal of the other pieces of him he *did* share with her clear down to her soul.

'You hold back too, Gabrielle,' he said gruffly.

'I do not!' she said indignantly. 'You get all of me.'

'Maybe in this,' he said reluctantly. 'Maybe you give everything when it comes to making love, but in so many other ways you hold back.'

'Name one!'

'You won't accept my offer to help you launch your wines,' he said curtly. 'You refuse to accept help from the House of Duvalier, even though it would be of benefit to you.'

'Because of Rafe,' she said hotly. 'I know it makes sense to take you up on your offer, but the bottom line is that Rafe doesn't want to. It's his business too, Lucien, and I will not go against him on this.'

'But you will continue to push for his agreement to purchase a vineyard he doesn't want in a place he never intends to return to? How does that work? How does that benefit the business you built together?' Luc caught her gaze and held it. 'Why haven't you and I sat down together and sorted out a partnership bid on the Hammerschmidt block, Gabrielle? Have you even mentioned that as an option to Rafe? Have you contemplated cutting Rafe out of this purchase altogether and bringing me into it? No. You don't want to blur the lines of business between us either. Nothing to do with Rafe. *You* don't want it.'

'Neither do you!' she shot at him. 'You said so yourself. Never mix business with pleasure, you said.'

'And I have since had time to reconsider those words. I *want* to mix business and pleasure, Gabrielle. I want you in every part of my life, but I already know what you'll say to that. No, Luc, I couldn't possibly live at Caverness. No, Luc, I won't consider going into business with you. No, Luc, I don't want to be your wife. You don't *want* all of me,

Gabrielle, it's as simple as that. You only want the part of me that suits you.' He drew away from her then to sit on the edge of the bed with his back to her. 'And then you turn around and wonder why I hold that last tiny piece of me back.'

'No,' she whispered. 'No, it's not like that.'

'Then marry me,' he said raggedly, still not turning to face her. 'Buy Hammerschmidt with me tomorrow. Commit to me. All of me.'

'It's too soon,' she protested.

'Not for me,' he said and began to gather up his clothes. 'I'm heading home. I need an early night.'

'Luc!' She scrambled upright and snatched for the bed sheet to cover her nakedness. 'Luc, please…' He turned and looked at her, just looked at her, and the rawness of his pain nearly brought her to her knees. 'Stay. We can work something out. Some sort of compromise. A way of doing business together. A time line for…commitment. Something.'

But he shook his head. 'I can't deal with you in half measures, Gabrielle. I can't be civilised and reasonable around you. It's all or nothing. Always has been.' His smile was bittersweet as he reached for the door handle.

'We talked before about what we would do if our affair got out of hand. Well, it is out of hand, Gabrielle. It was never *in* hand, not for me. This is the part where you run.'

CHAPTER NINE

GABRIELLE didn't run. She slept fretfully instead and woke late the following morning. She rolled on her back and stared at the ceiling, wondering in all seriousness whether she needed to get up at all. If she denied the morning, she could probably attempt to deny what had happened last night as well. Just close her eyes and snuggle into the sheets with the scent of Luc all around her and pretend that he was still in her bed and that any minute he would wake and reach for her as he'd done every other morning for the past week.

Only he wasn't there.

Gabrielle closed her eyes, her mind awash with muddled images and pleading words. Marry Luc. Don't marry him. Buy the vineyard. Risk the business. Don't buy the vineyard. Take Luc up on his offer to buy the vineyard together. Restore it together. Live in it together. The list of options went on and on. Make love. Make war. Make Luc see that saying wait didn't mean that she was saying no to any of his offers. Go to Caverness this morning. Take her suitcase with her. Find Luc. Phone him. Just close her eyes, hope for the best, and *love* him.

Above all, tell him she loved him.

She glanced at the bedside clock and groaned. It was after nine. Wasn't there something else she was supposed to be doing this morning besides obsess over her relationship with Luc?

Heaven help her—Josien.

She'd promised to visit her mother.

Get up, said the little voice inside her. *Get up and go and see her, or are you too cowardly to do that too?*

'Yes,' said Gabrielle to the latter accusation. She felt fragile and weepy and too cowardly by far to go another round with Josien.

Maybe you could talk to her, said the little voice. *Tell her about Luc. Ask her advice.*

'No.' Dear Lord, when had she *ever* taken Josien's advice? When had her mother ever given her advice worth following? No. Far better if she wanted advice to talk to Simone.

Simone would understand her fear of all the steps involved in committing to Luc. All the tangled little threads. Simone *knew* what it was like to be asked to take an irrevocable step into a world she hadn't been raised to.

Simone knew what it felt like to refuse to take such a step.

Only Gabrielle hadn't refused. Had she? Gabrielle groaned and flung the sheet aside.

She needed to shower and get dressed and gulp down coffee and decide whether to go to the auction or not, and whether she would go and see her mother or not. She needed to get *up* and get going.

Damned if she was going to run.

A composed and regal Josien opened her door when Gabrielle knocked on it at a quarter past ten that morning. Josien didn't have anything to say as they walked down the corridor towards the kitchen. Gabrielle didn't have anything to say either. Wariness ruled Gabrielle's thoughts. She didn't know why her mother wanted to see her and she didn't particularly care. Unless it had something to do with Josien deciding to reveal to Rafe that some anonymous prince was his father. If that were the case, Gabrielle cared a lot.

Hans was making coffee in the kitchen when they arrived. Gabrielle took it in her stride and told him how she liked her coffee when he asked her, and let him fuss over her as he saw her seated at the small wooden kitchen table. He had croissants for her and a selection of jams, a selection of bread rolls too, still warm from the baking.

'Josien walked into the village for them this morning,' said Hans with a conspiratorial glance in Gabrielle's direction. 'She needed something to do while she waited for your arrival. Something besides fret that you wouldn't turn up, that is. Sit,' said Hans to Josien. 'She's here now. *Talk* to her. Tell her all those things you told me.'

Josien sat. But she didn't seem to know how to begin.

'When do you leave for your new position?' Gabrielle asked Hans, more to fill the awkward silence than actually wanting to know.

'Next week,' said Hans with a lightning glance at Josien. 'We've been offered the caretaker's cottage at the entrance to the estate to live in. It needs work. A lot of work. But I'm confident it will be quite comfortable by the time Josien and I have finished with it.'

'It sounds exciting.' Gabrielle smiled faintly at his enthusiasm. Another man in need of a challenge. He had a big enough one on his hands with her mother, but then, looking into Hans' wise and compassionate eyes, she suspected he already knew that.

It seemed amazing to Gabrielle that Josien had chosen a gentle man to be with. A caring man. All the things Josien was not. Maybe he could soften her. Maybe he could succeed where no one else had. She hoped so. 'A bold new beginning.' She remembered her own terror at leaving Caverness at sixteen, and the unexpected benefits that had flowed from her departure. She remembered what she'd been back then, and where she stood now. 'I thoroughly recommend it.'

Josien turned towards the bench and fumbled with some papers. 'I'm planning on liquidising some of my assets,' she said in a low strained voice. 'The Duvalier family has been good to me over the years. I have a nest egg.'

Gabrielle smiled politely. 'It sounds like you have your plans well in hand.' Some people did. Gabrielle was not one of them, however. Not today, at any rate.

Josien glanced at Hans, took a deep breath, and spoke again. 'I don't know how much money you'll need to buy Hammerschmidt but there's money here if you need it. One and a half million euros. If it would help.'

Gabrielle blinked and set her coffee mug down on the table with a clatter.

'I know what it's like to want to bring your own monetary value to the table of a wealthy man,' continued Josien. 'To want to be seen as worthy.'

'Oh, *Maman*.' Every criticism Josien had ever laid on her came crowding into her brain. One by one, Gabrielle pushed them away until only the blindingly obvious remained. 'You just don't get it, do you? I don't have to prove myself to Luc in that manner. He doesn't care for my wealth or lack of it. He never has. All he sees is me.' She met her mother's gaze squarely. 'That's the way love should be. Isn't it?'

'I thought…' said Josien brokenly. 'I thought I was helping.'

'I know,' murmured Gabrielle, close to tears. 'I'm so sorry, *Maman*. You and I, we never get it right. I never think I'm good enough for you. You never seem to see the real me, only what others might think of me. I want the vineyard for *me*, *Maman*. Not to impress Luc. Not because I want to build an empire. I just want to stay here and work hard and love Luc, and be me. That's all I'm trying to do.'

'The money's there,' said her mother. 'If you need it.'

Gabrielle smiled and blinked away the sting in her eyes even as she shook her head in despair. 'Thank you.'

CHAPTER TEN

LUCIEN woke the morning of the auction with his control stretched thin and his temper dangerously close to erupting. He didn't know where he'd gone wrong with Gabrielle last night, only that one minute she'd been accusing him of not giving enough and the next minute he'd been heading for the door. There'd been heated discussion about giving and taking. There'd been an ultimatum in there too, one he never should have delivered. That was the problem with ultimatums. They delivered it all.

Or nothing.

Simone wasn't about when he stalked into the kitchen and set the coffee maker to making coffee. He'd need to advertise for another housekeeper soon. Not live in, as Josien had been, but someone from the village who would come and go as needed.

Two people, perhaps, who would share the load between them and call in extra help when needed. Simone often railed against the maintenance that was such a necessary part of the upkeep of Caverness. Heating it in winter, airing it in summer, chasing away the damp and making sure it shone. For all its elegance and grace, Chateau des Caverness asked a great deal of the people who cared for it. Gabrielle knew that. She was right to be wary of it. Who the hell lived in a castle this day and age anyhow? Why did he need to? Maybe, with Simone's agreement, they could turn the chateau into their head office—centralise the House of Duvalier's management operations here, open part of it to the public, keep just one wing of it available for family, and go and live elsewhere.

A place where the ancestral wealth didn't stare down at a person from every portrait and tapestry. A place where a woman not comfortable with the trappings of old money would feel more at home.

Luc smiled humourlessly. Finally a reason for buying the Hammerschmidt Manoir that made sense. He and Gabrielle could have made a comfortable home of it. Oh, it was still a little grand, still a home that would require maintenance, but it would have been theirs. Not his, but theirs, and together they could have stamped their mark on it.

Except that Gabrielle had not been enamoured of that suggestion either.

Auction day today. He'd told Simone he'd meet her there.

It was the last place he wanted to be.

He'd made his bid last night. His bid for Gabrielle's heart.

And he'd lost.

Gabrielle was running late. She'd returned to her rented apartment before heading for the auction and had lingered there too long. Wiping benches that hadn't needed wiping, changing clothes that hadn't needed changing. Anything to keep from confronting the real issue—what to do about Luc. Gabrielle believed what she'd said to her mother. Luc cared nothing for her station in life or lack of it. He cared for her. Enough to offer up everything he could by way of helping her get established here. Enough to make her his lover. Enough to want to marry her.

Enough.

There were no parking spaces out the front

of the elegant hotel in Epernay where the estate agents were holding the auction. Gabrielle finally found a parking spot two streets away, and running slightly late became running alarmingly late. An auctioneer's assistant met her at the door, his smile relieved as he signed her in and allocated her a bidding number. He ran through the deposit requirements should her bid be successful and Gabrielle nodded dutifully and looked around for the one face she hoped to see above all others.

But she couldn't see it.

She'd gone to the chateau directly after visiting with her mother.

Luc hadn't been there either.

Not that she had the foggiest idea what to say to him when she *did* find him. It would depend on what she saw in his eyes. On what kind of opening he was prepared to give her. She scanned the crowd again, spotted Simone, and headed towards her. Where the hell was he?

Luc strode into the auction room with moments to spare, nodding to the auctioneer's assistant who hurriedly greeted him and pointed him to where Simone sat waiting, third row from the front, with an empty chair on either side of her. He'd thought maybe Gabrielle would be sitting with Simone but she wasn't. He spotted her on the far side of the room, standing with her back to the crowd as she stared out the window, her profile pensive and her arms wrapped around the waist of her sleek black business suit.

'Where have you *been*?' asked Simone as he took the seat beside her. 'The auctioneers have been waiting for you to arrive for the last ten minutes. They almost started without you. I almost started without you. Gabrielle's been looking for you too. She was hoping to speak with you before the auction, but then she went over towards the window to try and get better reception on her phone. That or to spare my tender feelings,' said Simone, the lightness of her words at odds with the shadows in her eyes. 'I think she's calling Rafe now. She's already spent the last ten minutes trying to call you.'

He'd neglected to recharge his phone last night. Just one more thing amongst the many things he should have done differently last night. 'Did she say what she wanted to speak to me about?'

'No.' Simone settled back in her chair as

the auctioneer began his spiel. 'Too late, brother. You'll have to speak with her afterwards. Looks like we're away.'

Gabrielle turned, startled, when the auctioneer cleared his throat and began to speak in that penetrating, staccato way auctioneers had of speaking. Deliberately fast, deliberately trying to force urgency into a situation that called for cool deliberation. Deliberately encouraging the reckless decision.

She hadn't been here in this crowded and claustrophobic auction room. She'd been a million miles away, sleepy and sated and snuggled up in Luc's arms. Reliving last night's lovemaking. Rewriting it. Omitting her stupid statement about Luc holding back. Instead she'd closed her eyes and breathed Luc in and then she'd slept and woken in his arms. No questions, no arguments, no tension. No this.

It was time to phone Rafe. She did so hurriedly, scanning the room as the auctioneer continued his spiel. Luc had arrived, finally, and taken his place beside Simone. Dark eyed and radiating tension, he looked dangerously out of patience with the world in general and probably her in particular. He looked her way with a question in his eyes and her heart began to pound. He didn't ignore her. He didn't cut her down with a glance. He wasn't smiling—there wasn't a lot to smile about—but the way was not closed to her; he'd given her that much and for now it was enough. Rafe picked up his phone and Gabrielle spoke quickly and quietly into hers. 'It's me. I'm at the auction.'

'Where are we up to?' he said, his voice calm and reassuring, an anchor in an ocean of uncertainty.

'They're describing the property. I'm looking at a slideshow of it now.' A very beautiful, well-put-together slideshow showing all of the benefits and none of the drawbacks of the property. 'Rafe?' she said tentatively, knowing full well that now was not the time to say what she had to say. 'He asked me to marry him.'

Rafe cursed in rapid dialect French. The language of his childhood, a language he rarely used these days unless his patience was being severely tested. 'And?' he said tightly.

'The auctioneer just asked for someone to start the bidding at eighteen million.'

'Let someone else open the bidding,' said Rafe, 'and tell me what you said to Luc.'

'I said I needed more time. Luc said he didn't. He offered to buy Hammerschmidt in partnership with me.'

Rafe swore again and Gabrielle held the phone a little further away from her ear as she waited tensely for him to stop. 'Did you agree?' asked Rafe finally.

'No. They have a starting bid of sixteen million.'

'Luc's bid?'

'No.'

'What do you want to do, Gabrielle?'

'Cry,' she said faintly.

'Not an option, angel,' said Rafe. 'What's the bid?'

'Eighteen.'

'Luc's bid?'

'No.'

The bidding continued, slowing to increments of two hundred thousand. The auctioneer spoke again and Gabrielle relayed his words. 'Nineteen and on the market.'

'If you want it,' murmured Rafe, 'I suggest you bid.'

Gabrielle nodded. 'Nineteen-two,' she said into the phone.

'Whose bid?'

'Mine.'

'You mean ours,' said Rafe.

'I don't know what I mean,' she muttered, perilously close to tears—optional or not. 'Nineteen-six.'

'Whose bid?'

Gabrielle's gaze met Luc's. 'Mine.'

'Lucien, what are you doing?' asked Simone.

'Nothing.'

'Yes, I gathered that,' she said with the patience one might afford a dimwit. 'Aren't you meant to be bidding?'

'Yes.' But not against Gabrielle. He simply couldn't bring himself to do it. If Gabrielle wanted the old vineyard, he would not stand in her way. 'I asked her to marry me.'

'Really?' Simone lost all pretence of not being particularly interested in the unfolding events. 'Fast work. I know you have history, but still… Very fast work.'

'I love her.'

'Yes, I gathered that,' she said dryly.

'I asked her to consider buying this place together.'

'Good idea,' she murmured, graciously neglecting to remind him that she had been the one to suggest that particular notion in the first place.

'She said no,' he said grimly. 'To both.'

'Ah,' said Simone delicately. And then, with the mysterious way she occasionally had of reading his mind, 'Maybe you rushed her. Maybe that was what she wanted to talk to you about. Maybe she's had time to think your offers over and she's changed her mind. Women do change their minds on these things, you know.' She eyed Gabrielle narrowly. 'I can't believe she didn't *tell* me.'

'Glare at her later,' said Luc. 'Don't distract her while she's bidding.'

'*Me* glare at her? Look at you! You look like you want to shove a poker through someone and roast them over hot coals. Smile at her, for heaven's sake. No, not like you plan to eat her. For goodness' sake Luc, where are your *manners*? Show a little control.'

'Gabrielle happens to think I have plenty of control,' he said, and tried not to think of a naked Gabrielle tied to a pole. 'She'd prefer I lost a little more of it at times.'

'Brave woman,' said Simone. 'Dangerous move. I did warn her, but she never listens. She never has, when it comes to you.' Simone slid him a curious glance. 'Are you planning on giving her what she wants?'

'Yes.'

Simone sat back in her chair and smiled widely at the world, resting her elbows on the armrests as she crossed her legs and set her sandal to swinging. 'It's amazing what people will bid when they want something bad enough,' she said cheerfully. 'God, I love auctions.'

'There's a new bidder,' said Gabrielle into the phone. 'A woman.' Gabrielle nodded as the auctioneer glanced questioningly at her. She nodded a second time and waited. 'Twenty million,' she said, feeling faint. 'Not ours.'

'What's Luc doing?' asked Rafe.

'Watching me.'

'Yes or no question, Gabrielle. Could you be happy at Hammerschmidt without Luc in your life?'

'No.'

'Stop bidding,' said Rafe.

'I think Gabrielle's reached her limit,' said Simone, sitting up a little straighter and losing the smile. Luc thought so too. Gabrielle was speaking rapidly into the phone, her brow furrowed. She'd already shaken her head at the auctioneer to signify no. The auctioneer was merely giving Gabrielle and whoever was on the other end of the phone with her—and that would be Rafe—time to confer. Gabrielle shook her head again. Another no. The woman bidding against Gabrielle began to look smug. But not for long.

'New bidder,' said the auctioneer. 'Gentleman at the back. Thank you, sir. Your bid at twenty million two hundred thousand.'

Simone swivelled in her seat to see who'd joined the bidding. So did Luc.

'Isn't that Daddy's old school friend?' said Simone. 'The prince?'

'Yes. Only he's not a prince these days. He's a king.'

'I didn't know he had an interest in vineyards'

'It comes and it goes,' said Luc grimly. What the hell was His Royal Highness Etienne de Morsay doing here? Why now? Why this vineyard? Luc didn't believe in coincidences. He didn't believe in fairy tales either. Etienne wasn't here to make amends. He was here because he wanted to keep Rafael from gaining a foothold back into Europe. What other reason would he have for bidding?

* * *

'There's another new bidder,' said Gabrielle, frowning into the phone as she stared at the man at the back of the room and tried to remember where she'd seen him before. Nicely built for an older man. Broad shouldered, well clothed—the man carried the unmistakable veneer of old and distinguished wealth. 'I feel like I should know who he is, but I don't.'

And then the distinguished-looking gentleman turned his head to look directly at her with eyes as blue as a clear summer sky, and then she knew.

If she hadn't been leaning against the window she'd have stumbled. As it was she struggled for breath as she tried to make sense of the why of it. What on earth was Rafael's real father doing bidding on Hammerschmidt? Surely it couldn't be a coincidence. Could it?

And then her gaze whipped around the crowd as the auctioneer announced yet another new bidder.

Luc.

'Luc just bid against him,' she whispered into the phone.

'What price?' asked Rafe.

'Twenty-one.'

The prince with Rafael's eyes bid again. Luc topped him. The prince bid again. And again, while she stared at this man, this prince, this monster, and watched him shatter any last hope she had of ever calling Hammerschmidt home. 'It's twenty-four five now.'

'Give Luc my congratulations,' said Rafe.

'It's not his bid.'

'No, but the final bid will be.'

'What makes you think he'll succeed?' Gabrielle winced as the bidding went up again, too high for comfort or for common sense. 'What the hell is he *doing*? He's way past his stop price. This is insane!'

'That's Luc for you,' said Rafe, grim amusement laying heavy on his voice. 'He never could see straight when you were around. You might want to consider marrying him, angel. He's buying this place for you.'

'Er, Luc?' Simone's voice came as if from a great distance. 'About our limit price...'

'What about it?'

'We've passed it.'

He was aware of that. 'Gabrielle wants the vineyard,' he muttered. 'And that bastard can't have it.'

'Oh. Well, then,' muttered Simone and settled back in her chair with a very feminine smile of satisfaction. 'That's different.'

CHAPTER ELEVEN

Luc watched, his body tense as he waited for all the players in this room to make their moves. The auctioneer and his crew were seeing people out. The auctioneer had shaken Luc's hand briefly, smiled broadly, and excused himself to make sure that all the other plump pigeons in the room knew what else he had coming up for sale. The auctioneer would get to Luc later, when Luc was ready. The wily auctioneer had no fear that the House of Duvalier would renege on the purchase.

Simone was mingling—graciously accepting congratulations on the purchase and cleverly disseminating the information that, yes, the vineyard would be renovated and returned to the proper growing of champagne grapes and that, yes, indeed, there would be work available and that people could drop their résumés off at Caverness, particularly if they were skilled local workers—saying all the things Luc should be saying and wasn't.

Luc had more important issues to deal with.

Gabrielle stood over by the window, looking hesitant and wary as she finished her phone call and slipped her mobile into her handbag. Her eyes were on Etienne but then she dragged her gaze away from the older man and, with a squaring of delicate shoulders, she turned to look at Luc. Her lips tilted but her eyes stayed sombre as she started towards him. Luc stood and waited, while blood thundered through his veins and he tried not to feel like a schoolboy caught doing something stupid for the sake of trying to impress a girl.

Or protect a girl.

'Congratulations,' she said when she reached him, and held out her hand for him to shake as she kissed him lightly on the cheek.

'Gabrielle,' he muttered, nothing more than a warning as every muscle in his body tightened at her nearness.

'Relax,' she whispered as her lips brushed his other cheek. 'You're only getting two kisses from me on account of this being a public place. Then I'm going to berate you for paying so much for that stupid vineyard.'

Luc barely resisted grabbing her by the

waist and dragging her against him. 'It's not going to make the slightest bit of difference. I'm still going to want you just as much as if you *had* kissed me again,' he said gruffly. 'Possibly more.'

'Something to remember for future reference,' she said and stepped away from him with a smile that slid straight through him. 'I need to talk to you.'

And he with her. But not here. There were far too many people watching them. One in particular. 'Later.'

'Now. Luc, I have my suitcases in the car and I find myself in need of a place to stay.' Her words were crisp but he felt her anxiety as if it were his own. 'I was hoping to stay with you at Caverness.'

'I'll make space in my cupboard,' he said gently. If he wasn't mistaken she was attempting to address some of the issues that had plagued them last night. Awkward in a room full of people, but she attempted it nonetheless. 'For your clothes.'

She still looked anxious. As if she wasn't quite sure he understood what she was saying. 'I have a lot of clothes.'

'Caverness has a lot of cupboards,' he countered.

'Luc, I need to talk to you,' she murmured. 'When can that happen?'

'I'll be tied up here for a little while longer.'

'An hour?'

'Longer,' he said. 'Why don't you head back to the chateau with Simone and get settled? I'll deal with whatever needs dealing with here—' his eyes flickered to Etienne '—and I'll find you there.'

'It's a big castle,' she said. 'I'm thinking we should specify a time and place.'

She was absolutely right. 'Seven o'clock?'

'Seven it is,' she said. 'Shall I dress for dinner?'

'No. You should eat beforehand. Food should not be a priority.' Fair warning.

'Where shall I meet you?' she asked. 'Or would you prefer to collect me? You being a thoroughly liberated Frenchman and all.' She smiled then, a wicked little smile just for him. 'You may collect me from your bedroom.'

'I'll meet you.' Luc smiled as he leaned closer and brushed her ear with his lips. A taste of her, and a promise to keep. 'At seven o'clock, behind Caverness,' he murmured. 'In the caves.' Etienne was heading their way. 'Go. Get out of here.'

But it was too late.

'Lucien,' said Etienne, with the hint of a smile. 'Not exactly a bargain.'

'Satisfying though,' said Luc, without the slightest hint of friendliness.

Etienne shrugged. 'It amused me to see just how high you would bid, but then if the property had fallen to me I'd probably have had a great deal of explaining to do to the treasury and that's never pleasant,' he said. 'It occurred to me, seeing you with the young lady here, that we might have been bidding with exactly the same purpose in mind.'

'I doubt it,' said Luc, but Etienne had turned his attention to Gabrielle. 'Well bid, *mademoiselle*. I strongly suspect you have more good sense than either of us. Etienne De Morsay at your service.'

'His Royal Highness, King Etienne De Morsay,' added Luc grimly. 'An old friend of my father's.'

Gabrielle said nothing and Luc contemplated stepping in front of her and blocking her from the older man's view. As it was he reached for her hand and twined his fingers in hers. Whatever she needed from him, whatever she wanted, all she had to do was say the word. Stay. Go. He would take his cue from her. Gabrielle glanced at him and sent him a tiny, grateful smile before lifting her chin and turning back to Etienne, her hand still firmly clasped in his.

'I never thought I'd live to see a woman more beautiful than your mother,' said Etienne. 'I have now.'

'I never thought to see an older version of my brother sidle up and smile,' said Gabrielle baldly. 'I hope never to again. What do you want?'

'I see you inherited your mother's charm as well,' said Etienne.

'You leave my mother out of this!' snapped Gabrielle. 'What do you want?'

'A phone number,' he said. 'A contact address. For my son.'

'You could have gotten that any time during the past thirty years,' said Gabrielle. 'You don't need me for that.'

'An introduction,' he said next.

'Not from me,' said Gabrielle.

'So like your mother,' he murmured.

'I am *not* like my mother,' she said through clenched teeth. 'I swear I will slap the next person who implies that I am. My *mother* has spent half her life considering herself to be of no significant value to anyone because of you. Not good enough, not polished enough, not rich enough or beautiful enough. For you. Whereas me…I don't care what you think. I know my worth. And I know yours.' Gabrielle speared Etienne with ice-filled eyes. 'Rafael already has a father, thank you. One he loves very much. One who loves him. He doesn't need you.'

'But I need him,' said Etienne.

'I really don't care,' said Gabrielle and turned her back on Etienne dismissively. 'Seven this evening,' she said to Luc. 'I'll see you there.' And with another icy glare for Etienne, she stalked away.

Luc waited until Gabrielle had gone before turning his attention back to Etienne. The older man was sharp. Too sharp for Luc's liking.

'She knew who I was,' said Etienne thoughtfully. 'You told her?'

'No.' Not entirely true in the strictest sense, but he would not discuss Josien and Simone with Etienne. Not now. Not ever.

'Would I be right in assuming that Josien told her about me?'

'No.'

Etienne sighed. 'It doesn't have to be this difficult, Lucien. I intend no harm.'

That was a matter of opinion. Lucien waited in silence. Etienne sighed again.

'And Rafael…does he still know nothing of me?'

This question Luc would answer. 'Rafael believes that Harrison Alexander is his biological father. No one has ever told him otherwise.'

Shadows crossed the older man's eyes and he looked away; Luc followed the direction of the older man's gaze. Gabrielle had made her way to the door and was speaking with the auctioneer. Simone was with her, and together they seemed bent on reducing the auctioneer to a blushing morass of flattered middle-aged manhood. A dangerous combination, those two. Luc would have to figure out some way of reining in the wilder schemes they were likely to come up with once Gabrielle settled into his life. That or direct them to his advantage. He predicted great changes to the running of the House of Duvalier in the coming months. Changes that would benefit them all.

'So like her mother,' said Etienne, and Luc returned his attention to the matter at hand.

'No,' he said simply. 'She's not.'

'I still think you and I were bidding for the

same reason,' said Etienne. 'You wanted to purchase the vineyard for Josien's children, *non*?' He smiled wryly. 'So did I.'

'Why now?' said Luc, echoing Gabrielle's question. 'All these years you've been content to watch from afar. Keep tabs on your son from a distance. He needed you when he was a child, they all did, but you never came. Why turn up now?'

'My wife died last year,' said the older man with a smile that contrasted starkly with the sadness in his eyes. 'She never bore me any children although heaven knows she tried.'

'I'm sorry for your loss,' said Luc curtly.

'As am I,' said Etienne. 'I remained faithful to the wife that had been chosen for me for thirty years, no matter what the temptation. She was a good woman, a fine companion, and I grew to love her.' Etienne turned those vivid blue eyes on him and the memory of Rafael's eyes stabbed through Luc. 'I'm dying, Lucien, and my wife can no longer be hurt by revelations of my youthful indiscretion. I have no legitimate heirs. I wish to acknowledge my son. There is the matter of succession.'

Luc shook his head and suppressed a bitter laugh. As a child Rafael had needed a father badly. And this man had stood back. 'My kingdom for an heir.'

'All I'm asking for is an introduction,' said Etienne.

'I can't help you.' Luc quelled the faint stirrings of pity he felt for this man; for the duty-bound prince he'd once been, for the solitary king he'd become. 'It's not my introduction to give, and nor is it Gabrielle's. It's Josien's.'

'I need your help,' said Gabrielle to Simone as together they dragged her two large suitcases across the gravel courtyard towards the kitchen door.

'You're getting my help,' said Simone as she hauled on the suitcase and shifted it another three feet closer to the door. 'Is this gravel driving you nuts? Because it's driving me nuts. Crunch, crunch, crunch, and weeds popping up all through it. I'm thinking pavers.'

Gabrielle was thinking surrender, but she took the time to make a detour for the sake of a lifelong friendship. 'Pavers would be good,' she said. 'Pavers would allow suitcase wheels to function. I need your help with selecting a wedding dress.'

'A what?' Simone dropped the suitcase

she'd been dragging, dusted off her hands, and smiled broadly. 'Simone is At Your Service,' she said. 'This day just keeps getting better. Luc can get these cases in for you later. Let's go to Paris.'

'Not a *Paris* wedding dress. An instant wedding dress. As in something from out of my suitcase that looks vaguely weddingy and virginal. I need it by tonight.'

Simone's hands went to her hips and thunderclouds gathered in her eyes. 'You're marrying Luc *tonight*?'

'I'm not marrying him at all at the moment,' muttered Gabrielle, sweeping past Simone and making a grab for the handle of the suitcase Simone had dropped. 'Let me rephrase. Tonight is a very important night for me. An all or nothing night. It may not *be* an actual wedding night but that doesn't mean a woman can't prepare for it as if it were one. I need a frock a man will remember with pleasure. I need my hair up so he can take it down. I also need a shot of courage. Possibly Dutch, preferably French.'

'You need to stop teasing me like that,' said Simone as she came up and reclaimed the suitcase she'd been dragging along earlier. 'You also need a bridesmaid. But first things first. Where's he taking you?'

'Nowhere,' said Gabrielle loftily and then went and spoiled her bravado by blushing like a schoolgirl. 'I'm meeting him in the caves.'

The caves behind the Chateau des Caverness had been used for many purposes over the years. During times of war they'd hidden people and their belongings, given them shelter and given them ease. So many names carved into the soft grey stone walls. Names of the people who had worked here and played here, names of the wines. Gabrielle had carved her own name into these walls as a child. If she looked in that corner she would find her name there, written in childish scrawl, all the more childish for being so carefully carved. A record of her passing this way all those years ago. A witness to what had passed between her and Luc all those years ago as well.

Gabrielle made her way along the narrow corridor, lit only by the occasional beeswax candle. She knew the way, knew exactly where Luc would be. The tiny grotto where they'd begun to walk this path all those years ago. The tiny ancient grotto with its shelves of old wine and its hundreds of tiny tea-lights nesting in the walls. The little room with its black wrought-iron door and its worn wooden table in the corner—the kind that had endured for centuries.

She wore an ivory linen dress with wide shoulder straps and buttons all the way down the front. Her shoes were cream too and her hair was pinned up loosely. Cool air parted before her, caressing her skin as she drew ever closer to the place where it had all begun. This wasn't about seduction and it wasn't about sex, although the need for both burned fiercely through her. It was about finishing what she'd started, coming full circle. Candlelight drew her through the last of the big caverns towards the little grotto, soft yellow light, and she let it guide her as she had let it guide her all those years ago.

He was waiting for her, as she'd known he would be, his clothing dark but not as dark as his hair or his eyes. He stilled when he saw her, every muscle in his strong beautiful body tense and predatory. What would she find in her lover this night? What would he give?

What would *she* give in order to be with this man?

She closed the distance between them,

stopping only when they shared the same shadow, when all she need do to touch him was sway a little closer. 'Always so still,' she murmured. 'So very careful around me.' She spoke the words she'd spoken seven years ago, speaking them boldly, speaking them true. 'They tell me you're a danger to me.'

'I am.'

'Why?'

'Because of what I want,' he said huskily. New words to replace the silence that had once been his only answer. 'Because of what I would give in return.'

'What do you want?'

'Everything.'

'And what would you give for it?'

'Anything.'

'Some might call that obsession.'

'It is.'

'Some would call it possession.'

'It is.'

'Some might even be scared of such a love. Such an all-consuming, crazy kind of love. But not me.' She walked around him in a slow circle, staying close, trailing her fingertips up and over the broad expanse of his shoulder, the base of his neck, more shoulder, and then finally his heart. If seduction was war she commanded a conquering army. If seduction was a duel her blade would have drawn first blood . But this wasn't seduction. It was truth. 'I want what you have to offer. All of it.'

'The deed to Hammerschmidt,' he said huskily. 'It's yours.'

'Rafe warned me you'd say that,' she murmured and set her lips to the strong cord of his neck. Lightly. Lovingly. Such a still and waiting night. The heavy expectant stillness that came before an almighty storm. What would she bargain? And what would he give? She pulled back to study him, her breath catching at the raw magnificence of this man in the flickering light of a hundred candles. 'I propose a partnership. A new company. Something sticky and entwined. Something that's not yours or mine. Something that's ours.'

'I accept,' he said.

'You mentioned marriage,' she whispered, bringing her fingertips up to trace the perfect curve of his lips. He did not reach for her, though he shuddered hard. So much control in this man, such perfect control. 'And I had to think hard about that. I worried what others would think. I wasn't sure I was worthy of you or of the Duvalier name and all that came with it. And then it occurred to me that you didn't care what others might think and neither should I. All that mattered was whether I loved you. And I do.'

'Marry me,' he said.

'I accept,' she replied with a smile Luc would doubtless learn to be wary of. 'There is…one more thing. All that formidable control when I'm naked in your arms. All that careful restraint when I'm burning up inside for love of you,' she said delicately as she traced a path from his chest to the formidable bulge in his trousers. 'It has to go.'

An unholy light crept into his eyes, a wild and challenging hunger that called to her and always had. 'Then make it go,' he said.

She started with the buttons on his shirt, slowly easing them from their holes. Then she began in on his belt and his trousers until they too sat loosely in place. His shirt came off and dropped to the ground. She left his trousers where they were. For now.

'It would help if you kissed me,' he murmured.

She expected hunger from him. She craved the dark edge of need he brought to their lovemaking. But the kiss he shared with her was different again. Better again, as he showed her his soul, a soul filled with such purity and sweetness that she prayed his kiss would never end.

'I love you,' he murmured as his hands went to the pins in her hair. There were only a few of them, carefully placed, and moments later her hair tumbled down for him in waves. He stroked it with his knuckles, threaded it through open fingers and finally, finally his eyes grew black with desire as he wound it round his hand and made a fist. This time the sweetness in his kisses gave way to a fierce and uncontrollable need. 'I'll never hurt you,' he muttered.

'I know.' Night, the household staff had always called him, because of the shadows on his soul and the fierceness of his passions, but he was *her* night and always would be. She did not fear his hunger, and never had. 'This time you ride the storm with me,' she whispered as she slid her hands in his hair and dragged his lips closer. 'I'll be your light-house.' She touched her tongue to the side of his mouth, darkly pleased when a groan escaped him and he trapped her within the circle of his arms. 'I'll be your guide, and you need to trust me.'

'I do trust you.' If seduction was a war, Luc's kisses reminded her that even if she did have a conquering army at her back, this man commanded the skies. She wanted him naked. She wanted him wild.

'Surrender to me,' she whispered as she called up the storm. And he did.

* * * * *

*Harlequin offers a romance
for every mood!
See below for a sneak peek
from our paranormal romance line,
Silhouette® Nocturne™.
Enjoy a preview of REUNION
by USA TODAY bestselling author
Lindsay McKenna.*

Aella closed her eyes and sensed a distinct shift, like movement from the world around her to the unseen world.

She opened her eyes. And had a slight shock at the man standing ten feet away. He wasn't just any man. Her heart leaped and pounded. He reminded her of a fierce warrior from an ancient civilization. Incan? She wasn't sure but she felt his deep power and masculinity.

I'm Aella. Are you the guardian of this sacred site? she asked, hoping her telepathy was strong.

Fox's entire body soared with joy. Fox struggled to put his personal pleasure aside.

Greetings, Aella. I'm the assistant guardian

to this sacred area. You may call me Fox. How can I be of service to you, Aella? he asked.

I'm searching for a green sphere. A legend says that the Emperor Pachacuti had seven emerald spheres created for the Emerald Key necklace. He had seven of his priestesses and priests travel the world to hide these spheres from evil forces. It is said that when all seven spheres are found, restrung and worn, that Light will return to the Earth. The fourth sphere is here, at your sacred site. Are you aware of it? Aella held her breath. She loved looking at him, especially his sensual mouth. The desire to kiss him came out of nowhere.

Fox was stunned by the request. *I know of the Emerald Key necklace because I served the emperor at the time it was created. However, I did not realize that one of the spheres is here.*

Aella felt sad. Why? Every time she looked at Fox, her heart felt as if it would tear out of her chest. *May I stay in touch with you as I work with this site?* she asked.

Of course. Fox wanted nothing more than to be here with her. To absorb her ephemeral beauty and hear her speak once more.

Aella's spirit lifted. What *was* this strange

connection between them? Her curiosity was strong, but she had more pressing matters. In the next few days, Aella knew her life would change forever. How, she had no idea….

Look for REUNION
by USA TODAY *bestselling author*
Lindsay McKenna,
available April 2010,
only from Silhouette® Nocturne™.